THE LONG WAIT

...ton Manor was the only home Tammy ...ver known—and the Allerton family ...d her as their own, but when she ...ed that her love for Dick Allerton changed from the careless affection of ...hood to the mature love of a woman, ...as heartbroken when Dick still treated ...s his little sister. When the final blow ...d she thought she had lost not only ...k but the only other thing that made ...earable, she was in despair.

THE LONG WAIT

The Long Wait

by
Patricia Robins

Dales Large Print Books
Long Preston, North Yorkshire,
England.

British Library Cataloguing in Publication Data.

Robins, Patricia
    The long wait.

    A catalogue record for this book is
    available from the British Library

    ISBN 1-85389-629-2 pbk

First published in Great Britain by Hurst Blackett Ltd., an imprint of the Hutchinson Group, 1962

Published in Large Print February, 1996 by arrangement with Claire Lorrimer.

Dales Large Print is an imprint of
Library Magna Books Ltd.
Printed and bound in Great Britain by
T.J. Press (Padstow) Ltd., Cornwall, PL28 8RW.

ONE

It was very hot. The August sun beat down on their faces as they lay by the stream, listening to the cool rush of water over the shining stones.

They looked alike, both in striped tee-shirts and faded blue jeans. There was only a half-tone difference in the brown of their hair, but Tamily's was curlier than Dick's. It was urchin-cut and suited her small, pointed face.

Dick's younger sister, Mercia, called them The Heavenly Twins. Of course, they weren't even related, but they were always together, always had been ever since Tamily first came to live in the big house at the age of seven.

'Ten whole years!' Dick said suddenly, turning on his side and running a finger along Tamily's smooth arm. He smiled suddenly, wrinkling his blue eyes unconsciously in a mannerism so familiar to Tamily that she never noticed it, though strangers always did. 'We've known each

7

other longer than we haven't!' he remarked ambiguously.

But she knew what he meant—she always did.

'Horrible little boy you were at eight!'

'No worse than you at seven—all skin and bones and enormous great brown eyes like a gazelle.'

'Was I?' Tamily mused. Funny, she'd never thought much about her looks then. Everything was too new, too wonderful, too 'different' for her to have spared a moment's thought for herself.

'I'll never forget the day you arrived,' Dick said, suddenly serious. 'It was the beginning of the summer holidays, a day rather like this, shimmering and hot and lazy. Mother came out of the house with Jessie on one side and you on the other. Mercia and I had been speculating for weeks about you and your mother...what you'd be like, how you'd alter our lives. We thought we were going to hate you! You were dreadfully shy. Mother pushed you forward and you shook hands with Mercia but you wouldn't look at me.'

Tamily laughed. 'Well, I *was* shy! And desperately nervous. It was quite an ordeal for me. To begin with, Mother had spent weeks telling me how to conduct myself properly. I was scared of your mother and father and so afraid I'd do the wrong thing. After all, I'd never been in a big house before and "titled" people to me were like royalty—I thought they must be completely different from anything I'd ever known.'

It was Dick's turn to laugh.

'I know! You looked at our garden clothes with positive disapproval. I suppose you expected me to be in a sailor suit and Mercie in organdie!'

Tamily scowled, although her eyes were still smiling.

'My position wasn't easy, Dick. I knew your mother had engaged my mother as housekeeper and that I had a job, too. I was afraid I couldn't do that job. Supposing Mercia didn't like me? And what did a "companion" do anyway? Don't forget I was only seven.'

'You were a stunning success!' Dick said warmly, burying his face for a moment against her warm neck like a puppy. 'You gave Mercia a new lease of life and everyone always says she made such a good recovery because of your patience and encouragement.'

Tamily thought of the girl she had now

come to regard as a very, very dear sister. At seven, the pretty fair-haired little girl had been crippled by polio and now, ten years later, although she couldn't take an active part in sports or ride, or even dance, she could at least walk and lead an independent life. Dear Mercia! So gentle and sweet and affectionate. Generous too. When Dick came home from his prep school for the holidays, it was Mercia who insisted Tamily left her side to companion Dick. 'You go and bowl to him, Tamily!'—'Why don't you both go for a ride—take your lunch and spend the day out? I'll be quite all right—I've got a wonderful book I want to read!'

Mercia had been confined to a wheel-chair in those days and at first Tamily and Dick had been reluctant to leave her alone. Later, when Mercia and Tamily were alone, she had explained to Tamily that it made her far happier to see Dick amused and occupied, than to keep Tamily with her and see him bored and lonely. In those very early years, Tamily would rather have been with Mercia. She wasn't good at boys' sports then and Dick was always shouting at her: 'For goodness' sake, bowl straight!'—'Can't you bowl overarm?'—'Butter-fingers!'—'You'll never make a goal-keeper!'

She knew very well that he put up with her merely because there was no one else around.

Later, of course, when Dick went to public school, he would sometimes bring a boy home for a week or two; and then he had no time for Tamily and she would spend the long, lazy days sitting beside Mercia's chair, sewing, knitting, or just talking about the kind of life they would like to lead when they were grown up.

Now Dick had finished with school life and was on the threshold of Oxford. He would of course be going to the same college as had his father, Lord Allerton, to read history. Unlike most of Dick's contemporaries, there would be no need for him to earn a living when he came down. Lord Allerton, although not as rich as his father, nevertheless was a very wealthy man by present-day standards.

What Dick really wanted to do was to farm and although his father was hoping that Oxford might quash his idea and that Dick might follow his footsteps and go into politics, Tamily felt that Dick would never relinquish the dream he had so often told her about.

Despite the heat, she gave a sudden involuntary shiver. Could Oxford change everything? Would he come back a different person, with different habits? He was still a boy, really, with a boy's limited horizon; and Oxford—as Tamily very well knew from listening to Lady Allerton's diatribes on the subject—was going to change him from boy into man; round off 'the rough corners', turn him into a 'polished member of society'...

Whenever the voluble Lady Allerton used these phrases, Tamily felt at a loss to understand their meaning. As far as she was aware, Dick had no 'rough corners!' His manners were perfect and quite natural. His voice was deep, well-modulated and always kindly.

The only knowledge she herself had of 'society' was of the week-end guests who invaded Allerton Manor. On these occasions Tamily was not included as a member of the family although Lady Allerton frequently called on her to arrange the flowers or decorate the wonderful long refectory table in the dining-hall. She had a great gift for arranging things artistically and Lady Allerton had been quick to see this. Tamily was also required to see that the guests had everything they needed in their rooms and to help Simmonds, the old butler, at cocktail times. But she did not sit down to meals with the family on these occasions.

Once Dick had asked her if his mother had expressly excluded her from these gatherings, but Tamily, strangely embarrassed, had lied to him for the first time in her life and assured him that it was from her own choice. In point of fact, she didn't at all care for the shrill-voiced, hard-drinking, smart society women who were Lady Allerton's friends. They all called one another 'Darling'; had identical fashionable hair-styles and to Tamily's way of thinking were far too heavily made-up and over-dressed for a week-end in the country. Mercia agreed with her and managed whenever possible to have a sudden desperate headache or pain in her back which Lady Allerton strongly suspected, but could not prove, was fabricated for the occasion.

The men, for the most part, were different. Lord Allerton was a good deal older than his wife and his friends belonged to the previous generation, which Tamily supposed would have been described as the huntin', shootin' and fishin' type. They came in tweedy suits with guns or fishing rods, with their favourite pipes and very often with their favourite gun-dogs. They were always beautifully mannered and courteous to her, in contrast to the women who seldom bothered to say 'thank you' for any little service she had performed. But what frightened Tamily were the young men, their sons, whom they sometimes brought with them. They seemed to her to be younger, masculine editions of their mothers rather than youthful copies of their fathers. They wore exaggeratedly well-cut suits, or alternatively in the summer gaudy Italian beach wear. Their conversation consisted entirely of the Riviera, the races, the size of their newest car or even the amount of money they had made on the Stock Exchange. They quite openly discussed their latest love affairs or described the girl they were currently living with—not always in flattering terms. They seemed so far removed from Dick as to belong to a different species and now with a twist in her heart Tamily wondered if this was what Lady Allerton meant when she spoke of 'polishing Dick up'.

Granted, most of these objectionable young men were in their late twenties and did not belong to Dick's generation. Tamily had invariably liked the school friends he had brought home. Was she to suppose, therefore, that Dick and his friends as they grew older would change into such objectionable human beings or could she console herself with the thought that they were a peculiarity of the generation who reached adolescence at the end of the war?

She glanced sideways and saw that Dick was lying with his eyes shut, his hands behind his head, so that she could no longer see the long brown fingers with their curious, square nails. With a sudden moment of understanding she realized that she knew Dick's appearance so well that were she an artist she could have reproduced him on paper with every tiny detail accurate—the way the short brown hair curled inwards to a point at the back of his neck; the way his eyebrows turned upwards towards his forehead; his mouth, wide and generous, following the same upward line so that even in repose it looked as if he smiled.

'I love him,' Tamily thought. 'It isn't the way I've always loved him, with a young sister's adoration for an older brother. I love him completely and wholly, as a woman loves a man.' The realization did not come as a shock. It was as if until this moment she had been blind and now quietly and calmly she had opened her eyes on a beautiful truth.

'How strange!' Tamily thought. 'When Mercia and I tried to imagine how it would be when we first fell in love, we always supposed it would come as some kind of thunderbolt, shocking us into a completely new set of feelings; our emotions would change completely, our lives alter, even our personalities would be transformed!' But this unexpected awareness of loving Dick—of having always loved him—was so different—it was like a soft, warm wave washing over the ridges of the sand and leaving a smooth, shining perfection in its wake. There was as yet no torment of wondering whether her love was returned, no agony of indecision about the future, no pain, no sorrow; only a wonderful sense of completeness.

Quite suddenly Dick opened his eyes and seeing her strange, far-away expression said:

'Penny for them, Tammy?—and don't say they aren't worth a penny or I shall do what I did yesterday and duck you in the stream.'

For a moment Tamily couldn't reply to him. It seemed strange that Dick could be using the same teasing voice, the familiar words and the threats, when somewhere deep inside her everything had changed. Instinctively she knew that she must not let him guess how she felt. To do so might destroy the wonderfully easy, intimate companionship they shared. She forced herself to look at him and to say lightly:

'Oh, I was just wondering about Oxford. Whether it would change you. I expect you are looking forward to it, aren't you?'

Dick lay back on his arms again and stared into the brilliant blue of the sky as he pondered her question.

'I suppose I am rather excited, and yet on a glorious day like this who could possibly wish for anything better than to be lying here, contemplating the universe. Isn't it a gorgeous day, Tamily. We really ought to make the effort to swim. Blasted nuisance we forgot our costumes. Still, I suppose we could swim without them. Remember the last time we did, Tammy? Must have been about two years ago when we were on holiday in Cornwall. We decided to have a midnight, moonlight picnic on the beach and it was so warm, we had that gorgeous swim afterwards. We've had a lot of wonderful times as kids, haven't we? In a way I hate the thought of growing up and having to behave properly, yet we used to think that to be grown up meant the beginning of freedom and the end of restrictions. Funny how one's ideas become reversed as the years go by.'

He turned suddenly towards her and picking a blade of grass ran it gently down the bridge of her nose.

'You'll come to "Commem", won't you, Tammy? I'd like Mercia to come too but I suppose it wouldn't be much fun for her if she can't dance. Still, I intend to throw some parties while I'm up and I promise to be a good brother and find some really handsome young men for you both.'

Tamily sat up abruptly, stung into the first pain of loving where love was not returned. It amazed her to think that Dick could not possibly know how much his remarks hurt her, and yet she was forced to admit that only half an hour ago her reply would probably have been 'Mind you pick a dark-haired man for me. I don't like blonds.'

'I think we ought to go home,' she said, jumping up and brushing the patched seat of her jeans free from dried grass. 'Your mother has guests tonight and I want to have plenty of time to do the dinner-table.'

Dick got slowly to his feet and sighed.

'Blasted nuisance!' he said. 'I'd thought we might have a game of tennis after supper when it's cooler. I do wish Mother wouldn't be so wildly social. I'm sure Father doesn't like it any better than I do and it only makes a lot more work for you and Jess and the servants. How Mother keeps her staff, I don't know! I suppose she must pay them a staggering salary, or they'd never endure it.'

He linked his arm through hers and strolled with her across the ten-acre paddock that separated the trout stream from the formal gardens.

'As a matter of interest, Tamily, I hope she gives you a decent allowance?'

Tamily flushed, for the first time in her life aware of the social differences between herself and Dick. Her position at Allerton Manor was a strange one. Lady Allerton had engaged her mother as housekeeper and at the same time the seven-year-old Tamily was to act as Mercia's companion. No doubt her mother's salary had taken Tamily's uses into consideration. Because of her disablement, Mercia hadn't been able to go to school and a private governess had educated both girls. Their bedrooms were side by side and identical, and Tamily shared Mercia's life as if she were her real sister.

Tamily being the smaller of the two, it had become the natural thing for Mercia's last year's clothes to be handed down and once in a while Lady Allerton had herself bought Tamily new clothes from the same expensive shop in London for the occasions when Tamily was to accompany Merica outside the Manor.

The years had gone by simply, easily, happily, for all of them. A few months ago, on her seventeenth birthday, her mother had told her that Lady Allerton felt Tamily should now receive her own dress allowance in return for which she would act rather in the capacity of personal secretary to Lady Allerton. Until then, her duties in the house had been confined to the floral decoration, but now that she was old enough Lady Allerton wished her to take over such things as the seating arrangements for her guests and similar duties. It was Lady Allerton's wish that Tamily should look smart, though not ostentatious; and for this reason her allowance was a generous one.

She had accepted it gratefully, glad that she could now afford to buy her mother, Dick and Mercia birthday and Christmas presents from her own earnings; that she could afford little gifts for Mercia, who all their childhood whenever out shopping had never failed to bring something back for her.

Now Dick's question had made her see her true position in the household; she was an employee and as such must never expect Dick or Mercia to include her in their lives. Nothing and no one could stop her loving Dick, but she saw in this moment how completely hopeless such a love must always be. As Lord Allerton's heir, Dick would marry someone of his own social standing, someone who would in time become Lady Allerton and own Allerton Manor. She, Tamily, had no rights here, no place here, and the fact that she loved the glorious old Elizabethan manor house, and that it was the only home she knew, could not alter the fact that she lived here only so long as Lady Allerton chose. Quite possibly the day Mercia married and left home would mean she, too, must go.

They had reached the gate into the spinney, across the field now spread with the brilliant carpet of buttercups. The slight breath of a breeze brought to Tamily the intoxicating smell of roses from the rose garden beyond. It was all so beautiful, too beautiful. Tamily felt the hot tears sting her eyes and without warning she pulled her arm away from Dick and ran from him through the trees across the lawn and into the cool sanctuary of the house. One of the dogs barked and yapped at her heels as she sped up the wide thickly-carpeted stairway along the landing and into her room. In a wild, unreasonable panic she locked her door and flung herself on to her bed, burying her burning face against the cool silk. A moment later the door-knob rattled and Dick's voice, breathless and puzzled, called to her:

'What on earth are you up to, Tammy? Open this door this very minute. That's the first time you've ever beaten me in a race and you cheated. You never said one—two—three—go!...'

He broke off, waiting for her to come and unlock the door, but she couldn't. She clung to the eiderdown as if it were a raft at sea.

'Tammy, you little beast. Answer me!'

She forced herself to speak: 'Go away, Dick, I'm changing.'

The cool, level tone of her own voice surprised her. She heard Dick's laugh, easy, friendly.

'All right, my girl. I'll deal with you later.'

She heard the footsteps thudding boyishly down the stairs. Slowly she got off the bed and walked across to the door. She clenched her hands against the warm oak panels and, a child again, cried:

'It isn't fair...it just isn't fair.'

23

TWO

Tamily looked cool and poised as she arranged the delicate glass bowls of roses down the long length of the dining-table. The beautiful Georgian silver which had been in Lord Allerton's family for generations gleamed against the shining dark wood. Presently, when the candles were lit a thousand dancing lights would reflect in the highly polished surface and flash against the crystal glass-ware that Tamily well knew to be almost priceless.

She had grown up amongst the many beautiful heirlooms and possessions of the Allerton family and in one way she took them for granted, yet her mind, always sensitive to beauty, appreciated their loveliness as her hands moved skilfully along the table.

Beneath the sun-tan her skin was pale with a nervousness which was utterly foreign to her. She knew that presently she must come face to face with Dick and that her carefully formed composure might give way if she were not very careful. For once, she blessed the unbroken rule which meant she need not sit through the long four-course dinner that would presently be served. Once the dinner-gong had sounded, she could retire to her own room, away from the noise and laughter and from Dick's casually affectionate voice. She turned suddenly, hearing footsteps behind her, but it was only Mercia looking very young and adorable in a dead-white organza dress that billowed out in a skirt almost crinoline in its fullness. Despite the wonderful summer sunshine in which they had all been basking, Mercia's skin was still camelia-white and she looked to Tamily like a painting of some very beautiful young girl from the Victorian era.

'You look lovely, darling!' she said warmly, 'I've never seen you look prettier.'

Mercia gave her gentle smile.

'There must be something in the air then, because I was going to say the same to you, Tamily. That's the new dress, isn't it? It's terribly smart. When you showed it to me last week I thought it looked a little old for you but now I can see how right you were.'

She stood back to admire the coppery

brown cotton dinner-dress that was distinctly Italian in cut and style. It had a large white pattern of camellias and a narrow *piqué* binding round the neck which was cut low and square across the bosom. There was only a tone of difference in the colour of the dress and Tamily's sun-brown golden skin. She seemed to Mercia to have grown up very suddenly—in fact she looked several years older than she had done earlier today in jeans and tee shirt.

To her surprise, Mercia realized that Tamily was beautiful—not pretty, but with the kind of Italian warmth and glow combined with an elusiveness which was apparent in the picture of Italian model girls. She had a beautiful, long, lean figure and yet was not angular.

Mercia linked her arm through Tamily's and gave her a sisterly hug.

'What I really came to tell you, darling, was that I've persuaded Mamma to let you dine with us tonight. After all, if I can bear it so should you, and Dick and I feel we could do with your support against the howling mob!'

Tamily looked at Mercia in dismay. 'Oh, no, Mercia, please—really, I'd rather not...' she broke off seeing the look of disappointment cloud Mercia's transparent face. 'It was sweet of you to want to include me but I'm sure your mother would rather I retired, as I usually do. After all, Mercia, I'm not one of the family and it's not right that your mother should be persuaded to accept me as such.'

Mercia looked at her, aghast. 'But Tam, you *are* one of the family. Whatever's got into you, all of a sudden? Besides, if you want to be literal, the other guests aren't relations, they're Mother's friends. There's no reason why Dick and I should not invite you as *our* friend.'

Tamily bit her lip. 'Mercia, please don't think I'm unappreciative. The fact remains, I *am* an employee here.'

Mercia frowned. 'Tamily, what's happened? You *have* changed. Has Mother been saying something to hurt you? Jess hasn't been talking to you, has she? Why, it's quite absurd to make remarks like that. *You* an employee? You're my sister—no true sister could ever mean more to me than you do, and I know Dick feels the same. Surely the wonderful companionship we've all had as children is not going to alter now just because we're growing up. If I thought so, I just couldn't bear it. You

27

are dearer to me than anyone else in the world.'

Tamily felt the unaccustomed sting of tears hot against her eyelids. How could she make Mercia understand what she herself had only just begun to realize, that her world and Dick's could not be Tamily's world any longer. It was different when they were all children, but now it was only right and logical that Lady Allerton should wish them to make their closest friends amongst the young men and women with whom they might make suitable marriages. Naturally, any two people as kind and affectionate as Mercia and her brother would wish to remain loyal to their childhood companion. It must be her duty to Lady Allerton, who had given her so many years' happiness, to keep that friendship within bounds. Mercia and Dick might make light of their father's title, of their birth and social position, but Tamily knew that even in these days it counted. She had far too often heard Lady Allerton discourse upon the subject.

Although she did not often let herself criticize the woman who had given her the chance to lead the kind of life that would never otherwise have been possible, a wonderful education and a place in her home, Tamily's innate honesty made her admit that Lady Allerton was a snob. Her treatment of the servants belonged to another generation, and Tamily's mother had often said that were it not for the high salaries and luxurious living conditions in the Manor, Cook and the maid would never have stayed.

Curiously, Lady Allerton's manner towards her housekeeper had been quite different. She treated her almost as a friend. It was Jess in whom she confided her various personal worries, on whom she called when she suffered one of her spells of migraine and to whom she frequently deferred when it came to a question of choosing a dress from her extensive wardrobe for some special occasion. It was almost as if Lady Allerton had greater faith in Jess's judgment than in her own.

Of course, Tamily knew that her mother was a gentlewoman. Only last year Tamily had suddenly begun to take an interest in her background. She had always known, of course, that her mother had come from a well-to-do Scottish family in the Highlands; that her father was a Swiss several years older than Jess, and that they had fallen deeply in love on one of those long deer-stalking holidays to which her father had been invited. As far as she was aware, her father had died before she was born and Jess had come to England away from the unhappy memories of her Scottish home, to start a fresh life with the baby girl.

There was no reason, therefore, for Tamily to consider herself socially inferior by birth to the Allertons. Jess's father had been a Laird and no doubt had Jess remained within her home they would have been more than well-off, but it appeared that the Laird had never forgiven Jess for running away to England and Jess had been too proud, when circumstances brought them to the edge of poverty, to go home. It was then that Lady Allerton had come forward with her offer of a housekeeper's job at Allerton Manor.

But last year, questioning her mother closely about her own relatives, she had been puzzled by Jess's disinclination to talk of them—particularly of her father and the circumstances of his death. She had said, briefly:

'It still hurts me to think of it, Tammy. I'd really rather not discuss it unless you feel you *must* know.'

Always tender-hearted, Tamily had not pursued her interrogation. After all, she would never know her father or her grandparents, it seemed. Little point was served in being curious about them. Her position in the Allerton family seemed so assured and matter-of-fact; she had not felt the need for the further security of an established background.

It was Tamily's sudden awareness of her feelings for Dick which had changed everything. Mercia was more astute than she realized in remarking it, although she could have no idea of what had really happened in Tamily's heart. Tamily hoped she would never guess the truth although one part of her longed to be able to confide in the girl with whom she had always shared all her heart-aches, all her happiness. Now a barrier had sprung up between them because Mercia was first and foremost Dick's sister and must therefore consider his happiness before Tamily's.

'Tamily, you're standing there in a day-dream. Are you sure nothing has happened to upset you? You look so strange. As if you're far away from me.'

Tamily brought herself back to the

present problem with an effort. She gave a little laugh.

'Course I'm all right, Mercia. I've probably had a bit too much sun. It's made me feel rather sleepy. Really, darling, I'd rather not sit through dinner—I do feel a bit light-headed; and besides, I've finished the table and would hate the thought of having to re-arrange it.'

'It looks perfectly beautiful,' Mercia agreed. 'If you're sure you'd really rather not, then Dick and I will let you off this once. But it seems such a waste, Tamily, looking the way you do and retiring to your room. You ought to be on your way out to some gorgeous party with an equally gorgeous young man to escort you.'

'I don't like "gorgeous young men",' Tamily said, laughing.

The sound of the heavy front-door bell broke up their conversation. The first guests were arriving, and Lady Allerton would require Tamily's help to look after them.

'Come on, Mercia. Time we went in,' she said, and the two girls walked side by side, a perfect contrast to one another, through the great galleried hall and into the drawing-room.

She had meant to go to bed, but a soft evening breeze was blowing gently through the open windows as she sat staring into the darkened garden—the first cool moment of a hitherto breathless, deathless day. Down below the steady wave of high-pitched voices jangled with the call of an owl from the spinney and the hoarse croak of the many frogs on the edge of the lily-pond beneath her window. She felt restless and far from sleep. Everywhere she turned she seemed to see Dick's young, laughing face, almost as if he were deliberately taunting her with that teasing twinkle in his blue eyes, that laughing curve of his mouth.

She had only had a few moments conversation with him in the crowded drawing-room before dinner. He had come up behind her and twisting her round to face him had said, almost with surprise:

'Why, you look stunning, Tammy. I like the dress. That ought to get the boys!'

She had pulled away from him and turned quickly, knowing that colour had flooded into her cheeks, trying to betray her into exposing her true feelings. Now, remembering, she was appalled with the thought of the difficulties that beset her, now that love had come upon her. How could she hope to hide that which lay in her heart, when the mere sound of Dick's voice, the touch of his hand on her arm, could make her blush like some stupid schoolgirl! Must she spend these precious remaining weeks of his holiday avoiding him? And anyway, he would never let her do so. In his unselfconscious, egotistical fashion, he wanted her there beside him whenever he had nothing better to do.

'Let's swim, Tam'—'What about a game of tennis?' 'I think we'll go on a picnic'—'I've told Burroughs to have the horses ready so we can ride this morning...'

He took her acceptance for granted, just as he had in the days when it had been: 'Come and bowl to me,' or: 'You be goalkeeper.'

She had never resented the demands he made on her—Dick's wishes were then, as now, her pleasure to fulfil, yet how would she be able to bear the long hours in his company when at any moment she might betray herself with an unguarded word, or a blush.

Tormented by her thoughts, she decided

suddenly to go out for a walk. Already she had changed from the new party dress into a cotton housecoat, and now with sudden urgency she pulled on the boyish jeans and crumpled shirt, as if by wearing them she might revert to the uncomplicated childhood of yesterday. She slipped quietly along the landing, down the back staircase, avoiding the kitchen quarters. The garden door by the flower-room was open and she ran out on to the lawn, her feet bare against the heavy dew on the grass.

Without conscious thought of direction she followed the same path she and Dick had taken earlier today. As she ran though the spinney the owl she had heard flew suddenly past her, disturbed by her presence. In the distance she heard the squawk of a cock-pheasant, settling to roost. She did not stop but hurried on across the paddock until she could see the silver band of the trout stream, flowing quietly past her, its voice soft and cool as it whispered over the stony bed. It looked incredibly inviting and, strangely excited, Tamily decided on the spur of the instant to plunge into its cool depths.

As quickly as she had dressed, she now flung off her clothes and dived into the water. They often bathed here in preference to the swimming pool, for the water was colder, cleaner, and as nobody ever came near, delightfully secluded. Now the cold stabbed at her with sudden shock, and she struck out swiftly with easy strokes, towards the waterfall. This stream was really a tributary of the Medway and even in drought conditions was always deep and swift flowing. In the winter months it could flood quite dangerously, and once one particularly rainy year it had even spread across the paddock and the spinney. They had had enormous fun that winter. Dick had constructed a ramshackle raft on which he and Tamily spent the best part of every day, sometimes as pirates, sometimes as shipwrecked mariners, sometimes as enemy destroyers!

Mercia, still in her wheelchair, had not been excluded from these games; they had brought her down as near to the water as they dared and made her the Princess to be rescued, a mermaid, or an enemy spy, according to the mood of Dick's fertile imagination.

Remembering these moments, Tamily knew a sudden strange cessation of pain. No matter what happened in the future, no matter whom Dick might love and marry, and however empty and meaningless her own life, she would always have these wonderful years to treasure. She had meant more to Dick then than his own sister. His schoolboy friends came and went, changing every term, yet his friendship with her had survived the years, despite the difference in their sexes, their ages and their school environment. His attitude to Mercia had been different. Rather charmingly, he had adopted the role of protector towards the little invalid girl who was only one year his junior. He was thoughtful of her in the way he never bothered to be thoughtful of Tamily; he never teased Mercia, never made her do anything she didn't want to do, and seemed to know when she was tired. Tamily he expected to hang on until he was ready to give up and go home—he treated her as an equal, and although sometimes she had longed to be protected as Mercia was, she had recognized his treatment of her as a compliment. It was to Tamily he went whenever he was in a scrape, asking her and not Mercia to help him out of it. Tamily he expected to sneak him up some food from the kitchen when his father had packed him off to his bedroom on a bread-and-water diet for breaking all the greenhouse windows. Tamily, to whom he had written from school:

Afraid my school report isn't going to be hot this term. Dad is going to be livid, I suppose, unless of course it gets lost. If you see the usual long white envelope on the hall table the day before I break up, you might shove it in the boiler, there's a good sport.

Tamily's mother had caught her in the act and she had been made to go to Lord Allerton's study and confess what she had done. Terrified, she had approached Dick's father, with whom she had barely spoken more than a few words in her life and admitted to burning his correspondence. What she had not admitted to was that it was Dick's school report she had burnt. Puzzled, Dick's father had tried to find out why the little girl had thought fit to burn one of his letters, but neither threats nor cajolery could elicit the truth from her. He let her go and Tamily heard later from her mother that Lord Allerton had questioned her, too. Naturally, Jess had told the truth and the result was that Dick had been

38

caned when he came home. He'd sought Tamily out afterwards, grinning ruefully, and said:

'Oh, well, at least we tried! Thanks for not sneaking, Tam!'

Ever since then, Lord Allerton had made rather a fuss of the little girl, and although they seldom met he and Tamily had become silent but good friends.

Tamily felt suddenly cold, as much by the thought that those days were past as by the water. She turned and swam quickly back to the edge of the stream.

She had barely finished dressing when she heard footsteps. Frightened, she remained poised, one arm still not in its sleeve, remembered the lurid tales of murder that seemed to have hit the headlines lately.

It was almost a relief to hear Dick's voice, saying:

'Good heavens, Tam, you startled me. I wondered who on earth it could be!'

She pushed the wet hair out of her eyes and laughed.

'You frightened me, too! I've just had a swim!'

Quite unselfconsciously, Dick slipped off the beach robe which was all he was wearing. The naturalness of his action gave

Tamily no time to turn away her head, and now that he was standing before her in the darkness she found herself staring at him as objectively as if he were a statue, a white marble statue of a beautiful young man. He stretched his arms above his head and staring into the water, said:

'Bet it's cold!' and then dived in.

Tamily squatted on her heels, waiting for him. Strangely, the shyness and embarrassment in his presence had gone. For always? She wasn't certain. It was enough to know this moment of relief and not to question tomorrow.

Within seconds, Dick returned and pulled on the rough towelling bathrobe, shivering.

'You might have warned me!' he laughed. 'Still, it was grand. I feel miles better! How I hated this evening!' He squatted beside her and pulled out a packet of cigarettes. 'Mercie says you funked it—nasty little girl. Though I can't say I blame you. How long have you been here, Tam?'

'Not long,' she replied.

'If you'd told me you were coming, I'd have joined you,' Dick said. 'I say, let's go back and raid the larder, I'm starving.

40

We'll scramble eggs and eat them in the kitchen.'

Once again, he did not wait for her acceptance. He linked his arm in hers in the familiar way and, content as always to do as he wished, she walked beside him, feeling the warmth of his body against her side. She was cold now, for she had brought no towel with which to dry herself and her clothes were wet. Dick felt her shiver, and said:

'You are a silly chump, Tam. Why didn't you say you were wet? Race you to the house!'

As she ran beside him, she realized that it was only this afternoon she had run the same path—that time running away from him. How incredible it seemed that not even a day had passed since she had fallen in love with Dick.

'I'll start the cooking while you get into a dressing-gown,' Dick panted as they reached the garden door.

'It's all right—it's going to be all right!' Tamily thought as she climbed the stairs to her room. 'I can be friends with him. There'll be other times like this...I can be easy and natural and have fun with him. Nothing has changed really!'

41

Yet as she stopped to brush her hair and add a touch of lipstick and powder, she knew that it wasn't true. Before today, she would not have worried how she looked—not in front of Dick!

But he didn't even notice her appearance. He greeted her cheerfully at the kitchen door with a grin.

'Just in time, Tammy. I've burnt the toast!'

THREE

Darling Tammy.

Thanks for yours. I was glad to know Mercia was better. Poor Sweet! She has had a beastly time with that throat. I think you ought both to get away for a few weeks—seaside perhaps. You must need a change of air, too, after ten days in the sick-room.

Seems awful to have been enjoying myself while you've had such a time of it.

Still, the fact is I've been hitting the wild spots these last two weeks. For goodness' sake, don't tell Mother, Tammy, but the fact is I've met a wonderful girl. You know what Mother is, she'll want her pedigree back to the year dot and Sylvie is not at all what Mother would approve of. I think you'd like her though. She looks a bit like you, dark eyes and sort of olive skin. She's frightfully clever and is in one of the women's colleges here studying languages. She's half Russian and a quarter Lithuanian and a quarter French—you can imagine what the combination is like—all fire and fun and ooh-la-la!

Sylvie is twenty but she looks a lot older. I suppose Continental girls grow up quicker than English girls. Her father is frightfully rich and she has her own Renault for knocking around. Comes in useful—especially when I take her back after a party. As you can imagine, we aren't allowed girls in our rooms after dark and they are even more puritanical in the women's colleges.

I'd like to bring Sylvie home for Christmas but am not quite sure how the family will take it. Can you fish around and see what they think, Tam? I know Christmas is usually a family 'do' and even Mother doesn't invite her gang then. At the same time, Sylvie has never had a really English Christmas—she lives in Paris—and she's not anxious to go home this year as her father is away. Her mother is in *the Argentine with her fourth husband!*

Life is pretty good although I'm finding it hard to manage on my allowance—in fact, I'm overdrawn! If you can lend me a fiver till next month, Tam, I'd be frightfully grateful. I've just discovered it's Sylvie's birthday next week and I do want to get her something decent.

Fondest love to you and Mercia and I leave it to your discretion to pass the news on to Mercia if you think fit, or withhold it if not.

As ever,
Dick.

It was a week before Tamily showed Mercia the letter. It had hurt her so much she had felt certain it would upset Mercia, too. Then reason had prevailed and she realized that since Dick's sister would hardly be jealous, the letter would not distress her.

Mercia laughed.

'Trust old Dick to start sowing his wild oats before he's been up a month. This Sylvie sounds quite fun, Tammy. I don't see why he shouldn't bring her back, do you?'

'Because I couldn't bear to see them

together!' Tammy's heart cried out, but her lips said:

'No, no reason. Your mother might like her!'

Dick's next letter was less happy.

Thanks a million for the fiver, Tammy. I'll pay it back, of course. I managed to get Sylvie a rather decent cameo brooch she'd seen in one of the local curio shops and admired. She seemed very pleased. The last week has been rather quiet as Sylvie has a French friend visiting her so I haven't had a look-in all week. Of course I know the boy friend is really just a son of one of her father's business contacts and doesn't mean anything to Sylvie but he happens to be rather what you girls would call a 'glamorous type' so I can't help being jealous. However, I'm not too miserable as Sylvie had promised faithfully to come for Christmas, and thanks a lot, Tammy, for your last letter saying you would make her welcome. Mother wrote, too, with a formal invitation, so we're all set. Can't you and Mercia rustle up a couple of boy friends so we can have a gay time? It's going to seem very quiet at Allerton after the hectic life I'm leading here. Longing to see you both.

Love as ever,
Dick.

'It sounds as if he's really fallen for her.' Mercia said to Tammy as she handed back the letter. 'D'you think it's going to be anything serious?'

Tamily bent her head more closely over the tray-cloth she was embroidering:

'Dick's not nineteen yet so he's hardly likely to think in terms of marriage, is he?' she parried.

She knew one of those all too frequent moments of longing to confide in Mercia. These letters from Dick which she waited for in an agony of longing, and received in an agony of despair, were sapping at her determination to hide her true feelings from Dick's sister. Only her new-found pride kept her lips sealed. Mercia wasn't to know that the girl who sat beside her had left her childhood behind. Not only had Tamily's love for Dick changed her, but something else had effected her almost as deeply. Tamily had discovered that she was illegitimate. It was Jess who told her so there could be no mistake and even while her own full quota of common-sense assured her that no shame attached to her, she nevertheless felt as if the ground had been swept from under her feet.

Her mother, loving her so well, had noticed Tamily's unusual quietness, the breathless way in which she poured over any letter from Dick, the quick flush that mounted to her cheek whenever his name was spoken, the way she would hurry to her bedroom with a letter addressed to her in Dick's handwriting. One evening, not long after Dick's departure for Oxford, Jess had questioned her directly:

'Are you in love with Dick, Tamily?'

The girl had not tried to hide the truth. It had been such a relief to pour out the emotions she had hitherto had to conceal from everyone.

'There is no hope for me, is there Mother? He'll have to marry one of his own kind.'

Quietly, Jess had told her that it was even more hopeless than she might suppose. She had felt it best to quash Tamily's hopes before they could really begin to take shape. The reason she had to leave home, she told her daughter, was because her parents had discovered she was to have a child by a man with whom she had fallen so violently in love. They'd written to him, of course, but the reply had been blunt and to the point—he was already married.

'You've no idea, Tamily, how puritan- ically-minded the Scots can be. More modern, enlightened parents might have tried to help and protect their daughter. I think my mother might have weakened but my father—*never*. The good name of the family was at stake. Don't forget, Tamily, that he was the Laird and as such held in great respect by all the crofters and ghillies, and indeed, by his family and friends, too. So I left home, went to London and had you. I suppose I could have had you adopted but I couldn't bear to part with you. Not only were you my own daughter, but the child of the only man I had ever loved. I hadn't been educated to a career, but fortunately for me I had a good singing voice. I managed to get a job on the stage. I expect you don't remember a great deal about those early days. The woman who ran the boarding-house where we lived used to look after you when I was working. She was very good to us because many weeks I couldn't pay her at all. Then I applied for this job and our circumstances changed completely. Perhaps I should have told you the truth before now but you seemed so happy and content and secure, I couldn't bring myself to admit the truth.

Of course, I did wrong all those years ago, but believe me, I have paid for it a thousand times since.'

Tamily looked at her mother, in shocked surprise.

'Does—does Lady Allerton know?'

Jess nodded.

'And Mercia? Dick?'

'Certainly not. There's no reason why they ever should. You mustn't mind too much, Tamily. Nowadays there is no stigma attached to illegitimacy. When the time comes for you to fall in love with some nice young man, it will not prohibit you from being accepted by his family. But with Dick it might. I don't mean that he personally, were he in love with you, would think twice about it. Dick's no snob. But one must remember he is Lord Allerton's heir and that his mother has high hopes for him. I'm sorry, darling, but I don't think she would ever sanction such a marriage.'

White-faced, Tamily threw back her head and shrugged her shoulders in a gesture of bravado.

'You're not to worry, Mother. I've known all along that it was out of the question even before you told me this. But...'

Her voice broke despite her determination. 'I can't help loving him... There'll never be anyone else...'

Knowing what she now did, Tamily realized there could be no relief in confiding in the girl whom, despite everything, she still looked on as a sister. A sister? Tamily thought bitterly. How shocked Mercia would be if she knew the truth. She could never tell her, never. Mercia was so good and sweet and innocent. She could never see the bad in those around her, would never understand how Tamily's mother could have behaved with such abandon.

But Tamily understood. She knew that if Dick needed her, it would be beyond her power to refuse him. The love she felt for him was completely selfless and she would have no thought of the consequences to herself if she believed Dick's happiness dependent upon such a sacrifice.

Recognition of these violent emotions deep within her made her afraid. Life had been so easy until now. The right had always been right, and the wrong had always been wrong, and she had known the difference. She had her own free-will to decide which course she would take. Burning Dick's school report had been wrong, but she had chosen to risk a punishment if it would help him. Even then, these uncontrollable emotions must have held her in their grip, for she had not hesitated to do what she knew to be wrong, since it meant Dick's welfare.

'So I'm like my mother,' thought Tamily, 'and like her I am proud. He'll never know—*never.*'

Mercia's quiet gentle voice broke in on the black thoughts that had crowded her mind.

'I suppose we ought to try to think up some young people to invite while Sylvie's here. Any suggestions, Tamily?'

'We don't really know any "nice young men", do we?' Tamily mused. 'Unless of course you count young Dr Parker, though he can't be very young.'

Mercia lay down her own embroidery and stared out across the wintry landscape.

'He's twenty-seven,' she said, as if thinking aloud.

Tamily looked at her with surprise.

'However do you know that, darling?' she asked.

51

To her surprise Mercia turned pink and said with unusual hesitation in her voice:

'I asked Dr Timms last time he came. Tamily...' she paused, playing about with the skeins of coloured silks on her lap... 'Tamily, I think he rather likes me. Dr Parker, I mean. What did you think of him?'

'I don't think I really noticed much about him,' Tamily answered truthfully. 'Thinking back, I suppose he's rather handsome.'

Mercia looked at Tamily, her eyes shining.

'I'm *so* glad you think so. I liked him such a lot. We had a long talk, you know. He told me he'd only been qualified a year and was so grateful to Doctor Timms for offering him a junior partnership. He's very ambitious and with all the new housing estates springing up in the neighbourhood he thinks Doctor Timms' practice is going to expand enormously. He's frightfully keen on his work and I'm sure he's going to be a great success.'

She stopped suddenly, as if aware that this rush of words could mean only one thing. She looked at Tamily almost shyly and said:

'I think I might be falling in love with him, Tamily. Do you think I'm absolutely mad?'

Tamily put an arm round Mercia's shoulders, feeling a great rush of protectiveness towards her.

'No, I don't darling. I think it's wonderful. Why didn't you tell me before? Of course we must ask him up so you can see more of him. When Dick's home there'll be every excuse. Next time he comes I must take a better look at him.'

Mercia smiled, contentedly.

'I'm so glad I've told you. I wish it were the Christmas holidays now. I know it's only a fortnight before Dick gets home but it seems like a hundred years to wait. Can you understand that, Tamily?'

'Far more easily than you would imagine possible,' Tamily thought, knowing that it seemed a lifetime since Dick had waved her good-bye at Paddington Station and that the days until she would see him again were crawling by on leaden feet.

FOUR

Because every instinct demanded that she look her best for Dick's arrival, Tamily fought against the temptation to change from the boyish drill slacks and chunky sweater into a flattering wool dress. To change would mean that she expected Dick to notice her; and she had no right to hope. As if he would be likely to do so when he was bringing home with him the girl-friend he obviously adored!

Outwardly, therefore, it was the same Tamily Dick had always known who went out to meet them when they drove up to the house in Sylvie's smart red car.

Dick waved a hand to Tamily and rushed round the car to open the door for the driver. Tamily watched as the girl climbed out, noting with a sinking heart the long, slender nylon-clad legs, the stiletto-type shoes, the skin-tight tweed skirt and expensive suéde jacket. Dick was right...she was very attractive...

'This is Sylvie,' Dick was saying, his arm

linked possessively in hers. 'Sylvie, this is Tam!'

'Your brother?' the girl demanded in faultless French, 'I didn't know you had a brother, darling.'

Dick shouted with laughter.

'This is Tam—Tamily! You remember, Sylvie. I told you all about her.'

Tamily felt the older girl's gaze travel from her head to her toes and back again. The look was disdainful. Obviously, Sylvie did not approve of trousers for women. Tamily felt the tell-tale colour rush to her cheeks but she held her head high and returned the scrutiny. Had Sylvie, she wondered, deliberately mistaken her for a boy in order to accentuate to Dick her own femininity to stress the contrast between Tamily's boyish awkwardness and her own poised sophistication?

'Je suis enchanté faire votre connaissance,' Sylvie was saying sweetly, holding out a tiny, slender, white hand, the fingers delicate and tapering into long scarlet points. Tamily was forced to present her own square-cut boy's hand, but withdrew it again quickly.

'I'm afraid I don't speak French very well,' she said stiffly.

55

Dick's cheerful voice broke in beside them.

'But Sylvie speaks English every bit as well as she speaks French. In fact, she can cope with six languages without having to think about it, clever girl!'

'Do come in,' Tamily said politely. 'You must be cold and tired after the long drive.'

'I'll leave the cases till later,' Dick said, linking an arm though each girl's in his easy, affectionate way.

He led them into the hall, where a vast yule-log was burning cheerfully in the great fireplace.

Sylvie gave her charming, tinkling laugh.

Mais, c'est charmant,' she said, walking over to warm her hands before the blaze, and then turning deliberately to Tamily she said in faultless English:

'I was saying how charming this is!'

Tamily was saved a reply by the arrival of Lord and Lady Allerton with Mercia. They crowded round Dick and his girl friend, glad to have him home, eager to welcome his guest.

Quietly, Tamily slipped away to the kitchen to tell Cook that they were ready for tea. She, herself, had bought the crumpets, the chocolate gâteau, the ginger-biscuits, all of which made up Dick's favourite tea. She helped Simmonds to carry the great silver trays through to the drawing-room.

Sylvie's high feminine voice rose above the others, clear, rather like the notes of a bell. As her eyes caught sight of the laden plates, she threw up her hands in a Continental gesture and said:

'But I never eat a tea like this. It would be ruinous to my figure.'

Despite herself, Tamily was not so long out of the schoolroom that should avoid a quick grimace at Mercia. Mercia met the look with a barely discernible wink. Neither she nor Tamily had ever refused something enjoyable because of the weight they might put on. They were lucky, in that their figures seemed to keep to an average weight without the necessity of dieting. But this brief moment of shared schoolgirl amusement was soon past for Tamily when Dick remarked:

'Surely your weight is the last thing you should worry about, Sylvie. You're as slender as a willow-tree.'

The tone of his voice was warm and admiring, and there could be no doubting that this girl meant a great deal to him.

'I must try to like her, for Dick's sake,' Tamily thought.

But some deep instinct very far back in her mind told her that Sylvie was not what Dick needed, even though he might want her. It was not jealousy—but something to which she could give no name as yet.

Lady Allerton, however, seemed delighted with Dick's choice of girl-friend. She was chatting to Sylvie animatedly. Dick, sitting beside Sylvie, proud and happy, could see that his mother approved.

But it was not in Sylvie's nature to give her time to any woman for very long. She soon turned her charming, oval face towards Lord Allerton, and although Tamily could not catch their conversation she heard Lord Allerton's deep, kindly laugh and knew that he, too, was ready to be enslaved.

But Mercia remained her ally. As they dressed for dinner she said to Tamily:

'I suppose one must admit she's frightfully attractive.' She gave a rather clever imitation of the way Sylvie would throw back her head so that the long dark hair swung across her face, and half closed her eyes as Sylvie did when speaking to Dick.

Despite the misery in her heart, Tamily had to smile.

'I expect you would be bound to disapprove of any girl Dick brought home,' she said in an effort to be fair. 'Because we're so fond of him, we won't think any of his girl-friends good enough.'

Mercia drew the brush slowly through her long, fair hair.

'You know, Tamily, it's hard to realize that Dick isn't really a boy any longer. He looks the same, acts the same, and yet he's different. I'd never really thought until now that one day we will lose him completely. It makes me afraid. I know that sounds stupid, but we've been so happy, the three of us, such good friends. Soon we'll be going our separate ways, leading our separate lives. I don't think I like growing-up, do you?'

Tamily understood Mercia's feelings only too well, but she knew that growing-up wasn't going to be so hard for Mercia as for her. Mercia would fall in love with some nice young man like Keith Parker, and there would be no obstacles to their marriage, no broken hearts, no pain. Keith would be coming to dinner tonight and Tamily had little doubt that the young doctor would fall just a little bit more in love with Mercia and Mercia just a little bit more in love with him. He had been up twice already in the last month and it was obvious to Tamily that their friendship and affection for one another was blossoming gently as they learned a little more of each other's thoughts, ambitions and ideals.

Soon Mercia would not need her brother—Keith would be her whole world. Maybe she would have no time for Tamily, either.

Mercia was staring at Tamily's back with a thoughtful glance.

'You know, Tamily, I've been thinking about you a lot lately. I suppose it's hopeless to try to make life turn out the way you want it, and you and Dick have been so much like brother and sister that I can understand why it hasn't happened yet. But I do wish you two could fall in love and get married. It occurred to me the other night as I lay in bed that this was the perfect ending to the fairy tale that our childhood has been. Tamily, are you listening to me?'

Tamily kept her face carefully averted and dared not trust her voice to reply. She nodded her head.

'I thought how wonderful it would be if Dick came back from Oxford and saw you not as a kid sister but as the lovely person you really are; and that you would see him as a handsome, young undergrad and fall madly in love.' She sighed. 'I suppose it's a mad idea, but it would have been nice, Tamily, if you and Dick could have been married one day. It would have made us sisters-in-law...'

'Don't Mercia!' Tamily broke in, her voice sharp with anguish.

Mercia looked up swiftly at her friend's back. For a moment she was puzzled by the unmistakable note of pain in Tamily's voice. Then her eyes took in the white knuckles of Tamily's hands, clenched at her sides, and she realized that she had somehow hurt her deeply. Always sensitive to the feelings of others, and in particular to those of the girl with whom she had shared most of her life, the truth suddenly struck Mercia as if a curtain had been lifted that had hitherto blinded her. Perhaps it was her own gentle awakening to love for Keith Parker that enabled her now to guess what lay in Tamily's heart. Tamily was in love with her brother.

For a moment, Mercia's reaction was

one of pure happiness and pleasure. It was so right, so much what she herself desired! Tamily would make such a wonderful wife for Dick. She knew him so well, understood him—the good and the bad, and such a marriage would be based on the firmest of foundations. But as the seconds ticked by, she began to understand that life was not, after all, a fairy tale. Here was Dick, back from Oxford, with the girl he was obviously mad about, and as far as he was concerned, Tamily meant no more to him than the fond companion of his school days. No wonder Tamily was hurt!

If she would only break down and admit the truth, Mercia thought, then she could comfort Tamily somehow, and perhaps help to bring her and Dick together. But it was all too obvious that Tamily wished to keep her secret and Mercia was too fine a person to try to force her friend's confidence. She turned back to her dressing-table and busied herself deliberately rearranging the bottles of perfume.

'Shall I wear the *Lanvin* or the *Chanel?*' she questioned lightly... 'I think the *Lanvin*—it's more mysterious. I do hope Keith isn't going to find Sylvie too devastating. Do you think I stand a chance with him, Tam?'

Immensely relieved by the turn of the conversation, Tamily relaxed and put an arm affectionately round Mercia's shoulders.

'Any man who preferred Sylvie to you, darling, must be either very young or very silly, and your Keith struck me as being a very sensible, level-headed person.'

Mercia gave a little sigh. 'I do wish you wouldn't be so stubborn in your refusal to join us at dinner. Mother and Father both want you and it's quite absurd for you to have your meal by yourself. After all, you have every other meal with us, Tamily, why not dinner, too?'

Tamily smiled.

'I shall obviously have to give way in the end,' she said, 'or I shall never get any peace on this subject. But not tonight, Mercia. It spoils a dinner-party if there's an extra woman. I promise I'll join you next time I'm required to make up numbers. There's the pre-dinner bell. If you're ready we should go down.'

Arm-in-arm, the two girls descended the staircase and went across the hall to the drawing-room. So far, only Dick had come down. He was standing with his back to the Adam fireplace, legs astride, looking to the girls very grown-up and unfamiliar, in a new dinner jacket.

But it was the same easy-going, friendly Dick who came towards them and said:

'How nice you both look! You know, Tamily, I've come to the conclusion you're a schizophrenic. In the day time you go round like a scruffy little boy and at night time you emerge like a butterfly from a chrysalis into a beautiful young woman. I'm not quite sure any more which is the real you.'

'The tomboy, of course,' Tamily said quickly, releasing herself from the pressure of Dick's arm lying casually across her shoulders. It had become almost as painful now for him to notice her as it was when he ignored her. But Dick had already forgotten her. He was saying to Mercia, eagerly:

'Tell me what you think of Sylvie. She's fascinating, isn't she? And quite amazing too—she's only twenty-one and yet she's been all over the world and met some incredible people. I must say I never imagined I'd meet anyone quite like her at Oxford. My preconceived idea of girl students could not have been more wrong. Of course, Sylvie isn't typical. She was telling me in the car coming down that she probably won't bother to take her degree. She's just filling in time until her father goes to America next year and then she'll probably go with him. He likes her to act as hostess at his parties when he's entertaining and I'm sure she must be an enormous asset to him.'

He sat down on the long tapestry-covered stool which stood before the fire and clasped his arms round his knees in a gesture that was familiar to both the girls. How many times had they sat here together on winter evenings, listening to Dick dream about the future. Then of course it had been... 'If I can play a decent game next time I might make the First Fifteen by Easter...' '...I've got to swot like mad if I'm going to pass my Common Entrance...' '...Who'll hear my Latin verbs?'

Surprisingly, Dick had not only passed his exams, but to Lord Allerton's amazement he'd won a Minor Scholarship to his Public School.

'Sylvie says America is the most exciting place in the world to live. She said she'd invite me out to New York for the long vac. I wonder if Father would cough up the necessary for my fare? Which reminds me, Tammy, I owe you a fiver, don't I?'

'I very much hope *not*, Dick,' said a voice from the doorway. 'I don't like to think of you borrowing from the girls.'

Tamily knew Lord Allerton to be unusually strict about such things. There were codes of behaviour which governed his whole life, and all three of them had been left in little doubt as to what he approved and disapproved. Before Dick could speak, she said quickly:

'We had a bet and I won.'

'You bet a *fiver?*' Lord Allerton said, surprised. 'That's a lot of money for a wager.'

Tamily flushed. Lying never came easily for her and she had done so on the impulse of the moment.

'Oh, we're not serious,' she said. 'Sometimes we bet thousands of pounds but nobody's expected to pay up.'

This at least was true. Most of their conversation had begun with: 'Bet you a million I'll get there before you...' '...Bet you a bar of gold to a pound of feathers you don't catch this.'

Sylvie chose at this moment to effect her entrance. She had decided to exchange the simple *chic* of country tweeds for the sophisticated perfection of a white-satin sheath dress, which hugged her beautifully-curved body and shimmered sensuously as she moved.

Dick drew in his breath sharply, and jumping to his feet hurried forward. She gave him a long, seductive smile and said sweetly:

'I do hope I haven't kept you all waiting.'

'It's quite all right,' Dick said, although her remark had not needed a reply. 'Mother isn't down yet.'

'And so well worth waiting for, my dear,' put in Lord Allerton with his charming courtliness.

Sylvie slid past Dick and went up to his father.

'It's very kind of you, dear Lord Allerton, to invite me to your home. It is such a wonderful experience for me to see your lovely house and I feel especially complimented you should have allowed me to come at Christmas time, which I know you English keep very much as a family occasion.'

She paused to take a Martini from the tray of drinks Tamily held out to her and for a brief moment her eyes took in Tamily's changed appearance. If she felt surprised at the change in the young girl, she covered it quickly and said:

'Where is the oh-so-English butler who brought in the tea? I find him quite fascinating. Abroad, we do not have such a person, although in America they like, I know, this English tradition.'

'It's hardly necessary for Simmonds to serve the drinks when only the family is here,' Tamily replied politely. 'On these occasions I usually suffice.'

'Honestly, Tam, you make yourself sound like the second footman!' Dick protested, laughing. He turned to Sylvie and said: 'The trouble is, we all make use of Tam. She's so good-natured, we never have to ask her to do anything. It's done before you've thought of it.'

He shot Tamily a warm, friendly glance and she knew it was his 'thank-you' to her for getting him out of that awkward moment with his father.

Strangely, it was not until she had told that lie for him that Dick had realized his father was quite right—he should not have borrowed money from her. Somehow, Tam always seemed to him so much more of a boy than a girl and he'd always treated her as such. He must try to remember in future that she was grown-up.

Dear Tam! She was wonderful the way she always stood by him. In many ways she meant more to him even than Mercia. He must try to find someone really decent up at Oxford to whom he could introduce her. It was time she had some fun. She and Mercia had no idea, leading their quiet uneventful lives here at Allerton, what a lot of good times there were to be had in a place like Oxford. Girls were at a premium, certainly pretty girls like those two, and his new friends reckoned him to be lucky to have met up with a girl like Sylvie.

But he didn't need to be told how lucky he was. Although he'd been used all his life to the ready affection of the women in his home, he had never become conceited—indeed, he'd never asked himself why they were fond of him. Quite unconscious, therefore, of his good looks, his charming happy nature, he had wondered why a girl so stunning as Sylvie should allow him, a Freshman, and three years younger, to monopolize her time.

Dick might have been pleased to think that because of his height—he was six-foot-two—and broad, square shoulders, the age difference had not bothered Sylvie. He attracted her as a man and she found his shy approach refreshing after the uninhibited advances of Continental men. Dick might not have been so flattered to know that Sylvie was also impressed by his father's title. Although her own father was immensely rich, a good deal wealthier than Lord Allerton, in fact, he was a self-made man and none knew better than Sylvie the advantages of a title in the cosmopolitan world which surrounded her home life.

Dick had no idea, of course, that he was by no means her first boy friend. So far, his friendship with her had bordered on the platonic, with Dick innocently apologetic if their good-night embraces became rather passionate. Obviously, he respected her and it would not have occurred to him to suggest the 'affaire' which she hoped might be forthcoming. At the same time, she was still knocking around with Pierre Du Bois, and it was never really satisfactory having two lovers at once. She was bored with Pierre—tired of his particular brand of love-making. And Dick intrigued her with his sheer Englishness. His sense of what was right was a kind of challenge to her and already at the back of her mind was stirring a plan that would jolt Dick away from his carefully controlled standards of behaviour and into the wild passionate abandon of which she sensed him capable.

She had noted Dick's jealousy when Pierre had been visiting her at Oxford; had gauged the difference in his behaviour to her when Pierre had left. He had wanted to prove to her he was every bit as much a man as Pierre and no doubt if she had so chosen he'd have forgotten his scruples about the right way to behave towards the woman he loved. He was in love with her of course. It amused her to see how jealous he became when she paid too much attention to his father. He was so young, so new to the game, that she could hurt him with a word, please him with a look, rouse him with a smile. It was too easy, really. She was beginning to get bored. For her, love had no lasting benefits—it was like a new dish to be tasted, consumed, discarded, before she turned to something else. It was time now for their affaire to take the next step forward. No doubt, in this great big house with its innumerable passages and suites it would be a simple matter for Dick to come to her room. Pierre had never needed the suggestion put to him, but Dick's high-mindedness was what intrigued and challenged her. It must be overcome.

FIVE

It was Christmas Eve. Up in the old schoolroom in the left-wing of the house a fire burned cheerfully in the old-fashioned grate which still had its brass fender. Nobody had altered the room since the days when the children had done their lessons here. If anybody had cared to open the toy cupboard, school-books, exercise books, games of 'snap' and 'ludo' and Dick's stamp collection would probably have come tumbling on to the floor. Nowadays, no one came up here except Mercia or Tamily when they particularly wanted to be alone.

It had been Tamily's idea that Mercia should bring Keith up to the rather dusty, untidy, informal room. Downstairs there was all the hustle and bustle of a family preparing for Christmas Day. Dick and Tamily were hanging the decorations while Simmonds coped with the holly and mistletoe brought in by Burroughs the gardener. Sylvie followed him round, occasionally handing someone a drawing-pin or hammer but managing to avoid any of the hard work. Her high, bell-like voice rose above the normal level of conversation and when Tamily whispered 'Nursery' Mercia gratefully grabbed the straw of privacy held out to her.

She turned now to the man who sat beside her on the window seat and said:

'She has a wonderful nature, hasn't she Keith?'

With his strange ability to understand what she meant even when she did not express too clearly, the young doctor smiled and nodded in agreement.

'It isn't easy to be thinking of others when your heart's breaking,' he said quietly.

Mercia looked at him anxiously. 'So you guessed, too? I've known ever since the day

Dick came home. But Tamily is too proud to confide in me. I think she believes she has hidden her feelings successfully. Isn't there anything we can do, Keith?'

He put his hand over hers, and held it tightly.

'Thank you for the "we"—I think you meant it, Mercia.'

The soft colour stole into her cheeks; the linking of his name with her own had come without thought. She was too shy to look at him but he put his other hand beneath her chin and turned her face gently towards his own.

'You know I'm in love with you, don't you?' Keith said, more a statement than a question.

Mercia drew a tremulous breath. 'I—I wasn't sure, I hoped you might care a little bit. It has all happened so quickly. A few months ago we hadn't met. It wasn't...' she gave him her sweet, shy smile; ...'it wasn't at all how I expected love to come to me.'

He put his arms around her and drew her against him, laying his cheek against her soft fair hair.

'Then you *do* love me. Oh, Mercia, I hadn't dared to hope and yet I think all along, deep down inside me, I knew we belonged together. I wish I had more to offer you. It may be two or three years before I've really any right to ask you to marry me. Even then, I can't hope to offer you a home such as this.'

'I shan't mind, Keith. I don't mind waiting and I won't mind if we're poor. I know it's easy to say that if you don't really know what being poor means but if I can be with you, I know I shall be happy. I, too, wish I had more to offer. I'm not very strong, as you know. A doctor's wife ought surely to be able to work beside him. No, don't interrupt me, I've thought about this so much lately but I'm not unselfish like Tamily. I love you too much to pretend you mean nothing to me, though I know that is what I should be doing. I ought to be telling you that you'd soon get over the disappointment and find someone better, stronger than I am.'

'Then I'm glad you're selfish,' Keith cried passionately, 'You see, I *know* there couldn't be anyone else. It's as a wife I want you, Mercia, not as a secretary or a surgery-nurse—someone to whom I can go when I'm tired and irritated and want to forget all about my work. How could anyone looked at you and be reminded of test-tubes and prescriptions!'

She smiled with him, made happy once more by the picture of the future he presented. It was true that she could keep his home lovely, be there to soothe and refresh and encourage him—something he could treasure apart from his passionate love for medicine. She knew, too, that this was her only rival. Beneath the quiet, thoughtful exterior he was fiercely ambitious, dedicated to his work. She guessed that he had never meant to fall in love—not yet, anyhow. But it had happened and she would never urge him to hurry into a marriage for which he was not really ready. She, too, would like a little more time to grow up, to prepare herself for the break from home and the familiar way of life. Her acute illness in childhood had confined her world more perhaps than it confined Tamily's. She still suffered occasionally from acute back-ache and migraine, and everyone here took such wonderful care of her. Of course, Keith would take care of her, too. But she did not have Tamily's independent spirit.

Very gently, Keith kissed her. It was not easy for him to control his passionate nature, for like many quiet men he was passionate beneath the surface. But he sensed Mercia's timidity and it was this wonderful understanding of human nature which was making him such a good doctor. There was an instinct in him which enabled him to gauge a human being and know the fears, the limitations, the boundaries.

So he realized he must go very slowly with this young girl. Nothing must frighten or horrify her or, like a timid wild creature, she might flee beyond recall. She had led such a sheltered and protected life—even that attractive brother of hers treating her with protectiveness—that the world outside must seem hard, cruel, terrifying in her eyes. It must be his joy and his task to guide her through it, armouring her against cruelty with compassion, against evil with pity and against the hopelessness with faith.

With that one kiss, he dedicated himself to her. Then he slipped the signet ring off his little finger and gave it to her, saying:

'Let's not tell anyone yet, darling. It shall be our secret. In a little while, I'll speak to your father and we can become officially engaged. But for a while, I'd like to keep you all to myself.'

'Yes, yes!' Mercia agreed at once, her eyes shining. 'There'd be no peace if they knew—although I am afraid they might guess, Keith. I'm sure I must look different—I feel so happy!'

'You look radiant!' Keith told her, smiling. 'Perhaps it will be the excitement of Christmas that has brought the colour to your cheeks and the stars to your eyes.'

'Oh, Keith!' she whispered. 'I *do* so love you.'

He was rewarded by the spontaneous, warm pressure of her lips against his own.

'I think I'll *have* to tell Tamily!' Mercia said, as she leant back in the protective circle of his arms. 'I've never kept a secret from her...would you mind, darling?'

Keith smiled. 'No, of course not. Tamily would keep the secret. She's a fine person. I'm sorry things are not going well for her.'

Mercia frowned. 'It's almost worse now!' she said thoughtfully. 'I ought not to be so happy when she is so miserable. Oh, I WISH I could do something. I HATE that girl Sylvie!'

Keith laughed out aloud. 'Miaow! You can't exactly blame poor Dick. She's really quite an eyeful!' Seeing Mercia's pout, he tweaked her hair and laughed again. 'Silly! As if she could ever mean anything to me! All the same, I CAN see her attractions. But I shouldn't worry, darling. I don't think she's the marrying type. She may break a few corners off Dick's heart but that's all.'

Mercia brightened. 'If that's what you truly believe, then he might turn to Tamily on the rebound.'

'I hope not!' Keith said sincerely. 'That isn't the kind of love she will want from him. The danger is, she would probably take it. No, he'd have to fall in love with her completely and absolutely. Tamily isn't a girl for half measures—at least, I doubt it.'

'Why can't he see NOW that she's worth ten of Sylvie?' Mercia cried. 'After all, he's known Tamily all his life...he ought to know her worth.'

'It's just because he's been so close to her. It's a pity she can't go away for a while...'

'Go away? Tamily? But this is her home!' Mercia cried.

Keith shrugged. 'I know, and she is as much part of Allerton Manor as the fireside rug or the Adam fireplace.'

'Keith!' Mercia was horrified. 'You don't think we take her for granted?'

'No, dearest, not you! But the others, perhaps. Your mother and father certainly, and Dick most definitely. Whenever he wants something, it's "Tammy, could you get it?" or "Tam, be a dear and chuck my pipe over here!" Can you imagine doing that to a perfectly strange young woman? Of course not! Tamily is just his kid sister.'

'Then I'll talk to him—make him see for himself...'

'You can't do that, Mercia. If Tamily knew, she would never forgive you. The chances are, Dick would be terribly embarrassed and Tamily would lose what little she has. You can't make a man fall in love. He's got to do it for himself. Tamily might succeed, but she doesn't seem to try. There must be a reason but I can't think what it is.'

'You mean she could dress like Sylvie—use that peculiar walk and the way she half-closes her eyes?' Mercia suggested artlessly.

'Oh, darling, no!' Keith said smiling, loving her for her innocence. 'That

80

wouldn't be Tamily at all. But she might at least try to make him notice her. Instead, she keeps as far in the background as possible, leaving Sylvie a clear field.'

'That's the trouble with being young,' Mercia said thoughtfully. 'No one tells you how to behave. Did I push myself forward so you noticed me, Keith?'

'As if you needed to!' Keith told her, his eyes twinkling. 'I · walked into the room—saw the most gorgeous blonde and fell head over heels. Since then, there hasn't been any other woman in the room but you.'

'You're teasing!' Mercia said, burrowing her head like a puppy against his chest. 'That first time you came to see me when Dr Timms was ill, you just poked about in my throat with that horrible spoon and said "Ah! Um! Interesting!" I don't think you even noticed me.'

'That shows how wrong you were, my girl. I went straight back to Dr Timms and said: "Acute Laryngitis and I can't have that girl for my patient—I want to marry her".'

'Really?' Mercia asked, delighted.

'Yes, really! And do you know what

Dr Timms said? "Laryngitis, eh? Well, congratulations my boy." I'm still not sure if he was praising my diagnosis or my choice of a wife!'

'I don't believe a word of it, but I still love you!' Mercia cried, jumping up and pulling Keith up beside her. 'Oh, I'm so happy, so happy, Keith! Will it always be like this? Shall we always laugh and love each other so much?'

'Always!' Keith told her. 'Even when we are quarrelling violently. As I've been married six times already, I am qualified to tell you exactly what married life will be like.' The smile left his face and he became serious once more. 'Darling, you look so very beautiful. Let me kiss you once more before we go back to the others!'

She came willingly and trustingly into his arms and this time she returned his kiss as ardently as he could wish.

'You're wobbling the ladder, Tammy!' Dick called down from his precarious position on the top step. 'Stop it, girl! You're doing it on purpose!'

'I'm not, honestly!' Tamily replied, smiling in spite of herself. 'It's you, wavering about up there.'

He turned round to look down at her and somehow between them, the ladder toppled and fell on them both. Sylvie screamed and shouted for help.

But no one was hurt. Dick, rubbing his leg, looked at Tamily, grinning, and said:

'Serve you right, my girl.' And then, more gently, 'You're not hurt, are you?'

'Only my arm, probably broken!' Tamily replied. It was strange, but lying here in a tangled heap on the floor, paper chains, drawing-pins scattered around them, was so reminiscent of other Christmasses. Dick, too, must have felt the pull of childhood memories for he gave a tug at Tamily's hair, laughing and saying: 'You did it on purpose, you did it on purpose, you did it on purpose...' until she flew at him, beating at his chest with clenched fists, incensed as any ten-year-old by his teasing.

He caught hold of her wrists and held her at arm's length, grinning.

'Little spitfire! Never could control yourself!'

'You let me go this minute, Dick Allerton. You're a beastly little tease. It isn't fair, you're miles stronger than I.'

'Bet you couldn't beat me even with one

hand behind my back,' Dick challenged.

'Bet I could.'

'Go on, then, try.'

She flew at him again, and they toppled backwards on to the thick Persian carpet and subsided into helpless laughter. Sylvie's shrill voice brought them to their senses.

'Are you both quite mad?' she asked coldly, staring at them with a mixture of unbelief and disdain. That any young woman could behave in such a fashion! So undignified, so unfeminine...and Dick so childish.

They were looking at one another, grinning like two children caught in some act of mischief and she felt quite suddenly, *de trop*. She determined to end this nonsense immediately. She turned sharply on her heel and flung out of the room without a backward glance.

'Oh lor, that's done it!' said Tamily. But Dick did not seem very worried. He lay on the floor, laughing and saying: 'I suppose we do seem mad to her.'

It was Tamily's turn to sense the link between them. She felt a moment of pure happiness. This Dick belonged to her. Sylvie had no part in it and never would have. She realized her nose was probably shining, that she had ripped the leg of her slacks, and that she probably looked a mess. It didn't matter. Dick was making no attempt to follow Sylvie. For the moment he was hers. He pulled her down on the floor beside him and ran his hand through the back of her hair.

'You're sure you didn't get hurt?' he questioned.

She became conscious suddenly of the throbbing ache of her bruised elbow, but it was a welcome exchange for the pain that had gripped her heart these last weeks.

'It's nothing, really,' she said.

He knew her of old, and taking her hand rolled back the sleeve of her jersey. There was an angry lump on her elbow which made him whistle with concern.

'You are the most inveterate little liar,' he said admiringly. 'This must hurt like hell. Go and find Jess. Tell her to put some witch-hazel on or something. It's beginning to look like a boiled egg.'

But she stayed sitting beside him, unable to bring herself to break the moment of closeness with him. As if he had never expected her to go, he said suddenly:

'Will you do me a favour, Tam?'

'Of course, anything!'

'It's this blasted fellow Pierre what's-his-name. I know what happened when we were up at Oxford. He completely monopolized Sylvie and I hardly got a look-in. Will you be a sport and try to keep him away from Sylvie? You know, fix the dinner placing, make him dance with you, that sort of thing. It's no good asking Mercie—she's so taken up with that young medico of hers.'

'I asked for it!' Tamily thought. She was so hurt that for a moment she could not give Dick an answer. Then she said:

'I'll do what I can, Dick, but I'm afraid I shan't be much competition to Sylvie.'

Dick sighed. 'I suppose not. But you don't look too bad when you're dressed up, Tam. Wear that brown-and-white thing you had last summer. You looked your best in that.'

'It's a summer dress, I can't wear it. I'd freeze.'

'Well, freeze, then,' said Dick. 'You said you'd do anything.'

She was near to tears. She wanted so much to be able to please him, but he was asking the impossible.

'But it's a cotton dress, Dick. Everyone would think I was mad, wearing it at

Christmas time. Don't worry. I've got a new red velvet to wear tonight. I think you'll like it.'

'Yes, but will Pierre?' Dick said, frowning. 'I wish to God he weren't coming.'

'It was you who invited him,' Tamily reminded him, with a sudden feminine desire to hurt him.

'Damn it, I know that. Sylvie begged me to do so. It was for you, really, Tam.'

'For me?' Tamily repeated, dubiously.

'Yes, you,' Dick replied. 'Sylvie thought we ought to be "even" numbers and I agreed. I'm not having you shinning off upstairs to spend a lonely Christmas. It was really very decent of Sylvie to think of it, but I wish we could have rustled up someone else and not Pierre.'

Tamily bit her lip. She felt humiliated and at the end of her tether. So she was 'odd man out'. She stood up with no little dignity and, white-faced, looked down at him.

'Don't worry,' she said again. 'I'll fix Pierre.'

She turned and walked swiftly out of the room.

For once she did not appear at tea. She knew that the famous Pierre had arrived and she was deliberately avoiding him. She had no experience in this task of claiming a man's attention but her instinct stood her in good stead. It was clear to her now that what men admired in a woman was not her willingness to please them, nor her companionship nor even her good will. If Sylvie were taken as an example, they admired the provocative, the sensuous, the ultra-feminine, and they wanted what they couldn't have. Well, no doubt this Pierre would be wondering what *she* was like, since presumably he knew he had been asked here as her *vis-à-vis*. Let her absence titillate his curiosity. Meanwhile, she had alterations to make to the red velvet dress.

SIX

Had he but known it, Dick could not have given Tamily worse advice. Pierre, too, was playing a game and he wanted Sylvie von Praline. It had been two years now since the thirty-year-old Frenchman had first noticed her. She had attracted him more than any other woman he had known—and there had been many. He was sufficiently experienced to see the kind of woman she really was and yet it was this primitive, shallow nature of hers which intrigued him. He set his net and in a little while had caught her but for the first time in his life a woman's physical surrender had not been enough. Sylvie, he learned, was as strong and skilled in the game of love as he. He knew he had no permanent hold over her and his desire to possess her became an obsession. He would even have married her but Sylvie wasn't interested in marriage.

He had suffered the humiliation of knowing that she had other lovers beside himself, and despite his determination he had returned to her every time she beckoned. This was his one consolation—that she might discard other lovers when she tired of them, but she always came back to him.

Although the invitation to spend Christmas at Allerton Manor had come from Dick, Pierre knew very well that Sylvie was behind it. As always when she called, he went, but this time she was not going to have it all her own way. Given the opportunity, he would let Sylvie suffer a few of the pangs of jealousy, let her know what it meant to sleep the night alone in uncertainty.

He had glanced briefly at Dick's young sister Mercia, charmed momentarily by the pretty blonde girl with her sweet smile and rather fragile beauty. But it must have been obvious, even to a blind man, that she was in love with the English doctor. When Tamily came into the drawing-room before dinner, Pierre gave a little secret smile of satisfaction.

Here was a woman! Here, indeed, was competition for Sylvie. This one had fire, the passion, the *je-ne-sais-quoi*, and with it the charm of an awkward girl.

'Enchanté, Madamoiselle,' he said as he bent forward over her hand. He was truly enchanted by the bright pink that rushed to her cheeks in so delightful a way as he held her glance.

Only the knowledge that she had never looked better kept Tamily moving, poised and calm, amidst the small group. The red velvet dress, draped skilfully across the hips and falling away at the back into a graceful train, had been worth the large amount of money she had spent on it. The bodice had been full like the great balloon sleeves, but she had altered it now, so that it fitted as closely as the skirt, hugging the firm lines of her bosom and tapering to her long, slender waist. It was simplicity itself and yet drew every eye in the room.

'Wherever did you find it, Tamily? It's gorgeous!' from Lady Allerton.

'You look charming, my dear,' from Lord Allerton.

'You look beautiful, Tamily,' from Mercia.

From Sylvie, there had been one quick look of envy, and from Dick only the one word:

'Smashing!'

Now Simmonds was handing round the drinks and Tamily could see Mercia and Keith toasting each other silently with their eyes. She knew their secret now and was happy for them both. The more she had come to know of Keith Parker, the more she liked the dark-haired Scotsman. He was the prop that Mercia needed, someone strong, reliable, kindly, to take care of her.

Pierre spoke at her side, interrupting her thoughts.

'It is so kind of the Allertons to invite me

to this beautiful house,' he said, his accent even more marked as he pronounced 'All-air-ton', rolling his 'r'. You must be so happy to live in so beautiful a home?'

'Yes, of course,' Tamily agreed, uncertain of her companion. He was quite unlike any of Dick's friends, nor was he like the young society men-about-town who came down to Lady Allerton's house parties. He was dressed conventionally in dinner jacket, impeccably turned out and handsome in a dark Latin-looking way. He was not nearly so tall as Dick, reaching only a few inches above her head. And of course he looked, and was, older. He seemed quite at ease in these surroundings and his manners were perfect, if slightly over-stressed. His very strangeness compelled her attention. She could not know that he was a type, prevalent enough in the cosmopolitan cities of the world, wealthy, dissipated, blasé and yet not really bad; merely caught in the useless merry-go-round of society life. Too many parties, too much to drink, too many women, too much money and no ideals to live up to; no faith in themselves, in humanity or in God.

'Pierre, ici un moment,' Sylvie's voice called across the room.

But Pierre did not hear, or pretended not to hear her call.

'Let me get you another drink,' he said to Tamily. 'Martini, wasn't it?'

Tamily realized that this must be the first time in this house that someone had carried a drink to her, waited on her. Rather bitterly, she savoured the Frenchman's attentions, continuing as they did by her side at dinner and afterwards when he brought her coffee. With a sense of relief she realized that she was not, after all, having to make the effort to keep Pierre's attention centred on her instead of Sylvie. He was himself making the running. Tamily dared not look at Dick. She felt she could not bear to see the satisfaction in his face, satisfaction that some other man should find her attractive. Of course, he could not know how degraded she felt but at least she could pretend to herself that Dick had no part in it.

It was Dick's idea that they should dance, or perhaps it was Sylvie's. At any rate, he and Keith were rolling back the great Persian rug over the parquet floor and Mercia was putting the latest Russ Conway on the radio-gramophone.

Tamily was drawn to her feet by the Frenchman.

'I'm afraid I'm not very good,' she said apologetically. 'It must be a year since Dick taught us the cha-cha in the schoolroom. He always said I was a hopeless partner.'

But she seemed to be moving with surprising ease in Pierre's arms.

'I think it is the teacher and not the pupil who is at fault,' Pierre was saying. 'You have the rhythm perfectly, Mademoiselle Tamilee. You follow well and you are light on your feet.'

Certainly Pierre was a superb dancer. He obviously took his dancing seriously, unlike Dick. And once, as she began to speak he silenced her firmly but politely, saying:

'No, no, the dancing should be in silence to be most enjoyed.'

Tamily gave herself up to the pure pleasure of movement in time to music. It did not seem strange to her that he held her more tightly now and that his cheek was against her own. Unquestionably, this made following much easier and they could move as one person. The dance ended far too quickly but Pierre was not letting her go so soon. He, himself, put on the next record, choosing a Tango and ignoring her protests that she did not know the steps.

'Just follow,' he said, 'it will come.'

She found he was right and she no longer had to think what her feet were doing. She heard Sylvie's voice as she and Dick swept past them, rather petulant, and complaining.

'Well,' thought Tamily, 'the Tango is hardly Dick's favourite dance and perhaps Sylvie thinks she would do better with Pierre. This time, however, she is not going to have her own way.'

She underestimated Sylvie's determination. When the dance ended, she came over to Tamily and Pierre and said sweetly:

'You must not let me monopolize Dick. I'm sure you must be wanting to dance with him.'

Common courtesy demanded of Dick that he should ask Tamily to dance when Mercia had changed the record. It was an old-fashioned waltz, something Dick hated and Tamily said quickly:

'Let's sit it out, Dick. I need a rest.'

He followed her from the floor without argument, leaving Pierre and Sylvie to whirl away together. They sat by the window silently watching the couple on the floor. Tamily knew how hurt and angry Dick was. It was not that Sylvie had no right to dance with Pierre but she need not have made it so obvious to all three of them that she had had enough of Dick. She wanted to tell him she was sorry but she knew better than to offer him pity. Surprising her, Dick said suddenly:

'What do you think of that chap, Tamily? I can't quite make him out.'

'He seems quite nice,' Tamily said truthfully. 'At any rate, he dances beautifully...' she broke off, realizing her remark was hardly tactful in the circumstances.

Thoughtfully, Dick took her hand and idly played with her finger tips.

'He seems pretty smitten with you, Tam. You know you've surprised me this evening. I've never seen such a change in anyone. I didn't realize you had it in you to transform yourself—almost the ugly ducking into the swan. How *do* you women change yourself in a few hours? Beats me!'

Tamily gently withdrew her hand from Dick's and said lightly: 'A trade secret,

Dick. Make-up, perfume, things you probably know nothing about.'

Dick grinned: 'Not so sure I like you so much like this, Tam. You make me feel I ought to be rushing to get you an orange squash, or light a cigarette for you, or something.'

'I'll be me again tomorrow, if you want,' Tammy said in a small voice.

But Dick refused quickly. 'No, heaven forbid! You've been doing wonders keeping Pierre away from Sylvie. I'm counting on you to keep it up until he goes, Tammy, you don't think she really cares for him, do you?'

Tamily looked at the couple dancing cheek to cheek. Sylvie's eyes were closed and her face had a rapt, lost look which certainly had not been there when she danced with Dick. But knowing herself how well Pierre danced, it could be no more than that she was savouring the pleasure of movement and music. Maybe Pierre didn't mean much to her—just another man to be conquered in the way she had conquered Dick.

'I honestly don't know,' she said truthfully, 'I don't altogether understand her.'

'Nor me, neither,' Dick said, deliberately

ungrammatical. 'One minute she's all sweetness and I think she really cares about me and the next she almost seems bored with me. Perhaps I'm just not old enough to cope with a girl like Sylvie. The odd thing is she seems to like me best when I'm treating her rather badly.'

Tamily wasn't quite sure what he meant by those last words. She could not know that Dick was speaking of the night when he held Sylvie in his arms and lost a little of the control he was trying so desperately to keep hold of. It wasn't easy to kiss a girl like Sylvie and behave honourably at the same time. She could drive him mad with those long, searching kisses, her nearness, her perfume, her responsiveness. He had to force himself to remember that if she were his sister and he some other man, he would want to knock him down for harbouring the thoughts he had. 'of course,' he told himself, 'Sylvie had no idea how provocative she was.' It was up to him to protect her from his baser self. To protect her, too, against her own moments of weakness. Once or twice when he had known he must leave her, she had clung to him fiercely and begged him to stay. He never mentioned these moments to her when they met again, certain that she would be ashamed of herself.

Dick was no prude. The week Pierre had been in Oxford he and two friends had gone on a pub-crawl. They had ended up in a local hall and picked up three girls. Somehow, Dick had found himself back at the girls' digs and it had been daylight before he slipped into the College gardens and back to his room. But this had been different. The girls had obviously been waiting to be picked up and had not even waited until the end of the dance to suggest the boys went home with them. Dick knew from talk at his college that a group of these girls considered themselves all but College property and that the dance hall was a recognized place for picking up a girl for the night.

But Sylvie he put in the same category as Mercia and Tam. He idolized her with a boy's first love and he would have been shocked and horrified if he could have heard Sylvie's voice at that moment, whispering against Pierre's ear:

'Try to get along to my room tonight, Pierre. I'll be waiting...'

SEVEN

The little Norman church in the village of Allerton was filled this bright Christmas morning. The frost had cleared from the ground and a bright December sun had tried to find its way through the stained-glass windows. It lay in patches on the cold stone floor and dust from the hassocks curled lazily in the bridge the sunbeams made between door and window.

Tamily tried to concentrate on the old Vicar's voice. It was his usual Christmas sermon on the birth of Jesus in the stable, the words so familiar to Tamily that despite her intentions her mind wandered.

Beside her, Dick fidgeted with his hymn-book. His face was miserable and dark with his own thoughts. Tamily knew the reason. After breakfast, when presents had been distributed, Pierre had announced that he wished to go to Mass at the Roman Catholic Church in Barntree. Barntree was their nearest sizeable town and it would be necessary for someone to drive Pierre as he could not be expected to walk the ten miles there and back. Sylvie had offered to take him in her car.

'But you are not of my Church, Sylvie,' Pierre protested. 'I will manage with the bus.'

'I'm afraid there is no bus on Christmas Day,' Lord Allerton apologized to his guest. 'Benson, the chauffeur, could drive you in the Morris.' Sylvie, however, had insisted upon performing the task and Tamily had seen by Dick's expression how disappointed he was. He was not particularly religious but there was something rather beautiful about the simple, joyous service on Christmas mornings and she could appreciate his wish to share the occasion with the girl he loved.

The Vicar was announcing the last carol now and people were leafing through their hymn-books finding the page. The village choir was not up to much as a rule, but this morning, as always, the church was full and soon the voices rose triumphantly above the faltering notes of the organ.

Tamily saw Dick lift his head and his deep baritone voice joined in with the volume of sound. For a moment he looked happy, as if he had forgotten Sylvie and was sharing the moment of rejoicing with the rest of the congregation.

Soon afterwards they were out in the sunshine and Dick took her arm.

'Let's walk home, Tamily,' he said. 'I could do with some fresh air.'

On the way back, Dick cross-questioned her about Mercia.

'What's going on between Mercia and Keith? Is she in love with him? What do you think of him, Tam? D'you think it's serious?'

Tamily wasn't sure how far Mercia expected her to keep her secret. She prevaricated, answering only some of Dick's questions, telling him how much she liked Keith and that if it were to turn into something serious she could not think of anyone better suited to Mercia or better qualified to take care of her. Dick seemed relieved, as if Tamily's viewpoint really mattered.

'Funny how suddenly we've all seemed to grow up!' he said, thoughtfully. 'This time last year none of us had given falling in love a thought. Already Mercia and I are in the throes. I suppose you'll be next, Tammy. And while we're on the subject, you mind your step with Pierre. I was watching him last night and I think he's a lot too familiar. And what's so funny about that?'

Despite herself, Tamily was smiling. 'Really, Dick, you're never satisfied. One moment I'm supposed to encourage him and the next you're complaining because I appear to have succeeded.'

For once Dick's laugh was absent. Almost pompously he reproved her. 'For heaven's sake, Tam, surely you didn't think I meant you to take me seriously? I only meant you to try to keep him out of Sylvie's way, not to seduce the wretched fellow! The more I know of him, the more I dislike him.'

Tamily flung back her head defiantly. 'Well, I rather like him,' she said flatly and not altogether truthfully. 'And he dances beautifully.'

'And a damn'd sight too close,' said Dick, frowning. 'You watch your step, Tamily, and don't come crying to me for help if you find you've bitten off more than you can chew.'

Tamily was more indignant than hurt. 'I'm quite capable of taking care of myself, thank you, Dick,' she told him quietly. 'I certainly wouldn't dream of asking *you* to come to my aid if I need any.'

Dick was immediately apologetic. It was one of the traits in his character which always disarmed her—one moment he could taunt and hurt her, and the next show her with easy apology and affection that he'd never meant to do any such thing.

'Come off it, Tam. You know damn well I'd knock his block off if you asked me to—in fact, without your asking me if he misbehaved himself with you. It's because I don't want you hurt that I'm trying to warn you.'

'Dick, Dick!' she thought. 'When you know me so well, how can you know so little of what goes on in my heart? Don't you realize that no other man but you has the power to hurt me? It is against you I need protection! Will the day ever come when I can steel myself against my love for you?'

But Dick's thoughts were no longer concerned with her. He was wondering whether Pierre and Sylvie were on their way home. He would have been tormented had he been able to pierce the barrier of space to see them now. Sylvie had stopped the car in a quiet country by-road and was talking to Pierre in a low, furious voice.

'Don't make the mistake, Pierre, of thinking you can fool with me,' she said angrily.

His lazy smile infuriated her further.

'I mean it, Pierre. If you start something with that girl, I'll finish with you for good and all. I'm not the kind to be satisfied with another woman's leavings.'

She was speaking in French so that there could be no question of Pierre misunderstanding her.

He ignored her remarks.

'Don't you think we should return to our hosts?' he inquired with delicate politeness.

Sylvie's hands clenched white against the steering-wheel.

'Damn you, Pierre!' she swore softly. 'Answer me or I'll make you get out and walk home.'

He gave a secret half-smile. Sylvie was no different from other women. He ought to have seen this years ago. But he'd been too blinded by his passionate desire for her to play the game with his usual well-thought-out tactics. Now, by inviting him here to Allerton Manor, she had given him the opportunity he needed and he'd been clever enough to take it.

'Very well, chérie,' he said quietly. 'Since you insist upon an answer, my reply to you is quite simple. *I* no longer wish to be in the position of taking another man's leavings. If this Allerton is important to you, that is quite all right by me but I think he would not be very likely to approve if I had come to your room last night. Nor do I see why, if you can amuse yourself with him, I cannot amuse myself with *la petite*. I find her delightfully refreshing, you know. She has much of your appeal and the added quality that it is not shop-soiled.'

White-faced and furious, she swung round and slapped him hard across the cheek.

Pierre's mouth tightened. He caught her wrist and held it in an iron grip.

'Don't ever do that again,' he all but spat the words at her. Sylvie realized she had gone too far. Men like Pierre could be dangerous when provoked to such extremes. She was afraid, and yet at the same time the deeply primitive part of her nature was satisfied to know that she was powerless to move.

'Let me go, Pierre,' she said more quietly. 'You're hurting my wrist.'

She half expected this quarrel would

follow the pattern of others in the past. Pierre would sweep her into his arms, the harsh words forgotten in their love-making. But this time Pierre let go of her hand and said:

'I think we should go home, Sylvie. They will be wondering where we are.'

She wasn't going to beg nor would she let him see her disappointment. As she drove obediently towards Allerton her mind was speculating. What could account for this change in Pierre? He had ceased to be her adoring slave, ready to gratify her whims, satiate her desire, obey her commands. Had he fallen out of love with her? Could he be in love with that Tamily?

Seldom honest with others but always with herself, Sylvie was prepared to admit Tamily's attractions. The girl was unusually fascinating. She did not possess the golden blue-eyed perfection of so many 'pretty' English girls. Hers was a more Continental charm. The dark eyes, dark hair and creamy skin could be Italian, perhaps; the high cheekbones and full red mouth, Slavonic? And the combination of passion below the surface of purity and innocence might well have fired the imagination of someone like Pierre.

Oh yes! she understood Pierre well enough. Like herself, he had had too many lovers and craved something new. Dick in many ways held the same appeal for her as Tamily might have for Pierre. She had persuaded Dick to invite Pierre, hoping that a rival might have the required effect on Dick. Instead of this, he was behaving like a sulky schoolboy and she was beginning to find his jealousy boring. Perhaps, after all, she didn't care so much one way or the other. If it were not for the thought that if she played her cards right she could one day be Lady Allerton, she might push off with Pierre today.

With a sudden start, she realized that the dependable Pierre was no longer quite so dependable. He sounded as if he had meant it when he'd said just now he wasn't prepared to take a back seat whilst she played her little game with Dick. How would she really care if Pierre walked out on her? She was no longer sure. Cleverly, he had underminded her self-assurance. She was no longer sure *what* she wanted.

On her wrist was the very expensive gold charm bracelet Pierre had given her this morning on the way to church. Of course, he could well afford to lavish fifty pounds or sixty pounds on her. Pierre had a wealthy and indulgent father who gave him sufficient money to make a job unnecessary and for Pierre to travel and waste his time as he pleased. Occasionally he would represent his father's jewellery firm and this invariably brought forth a nice fat bonus. The bracelet, which might have cost anyone else as much as a hundred pounds, Pierre had probably bought for half that figure.

Beside it, Dick's powder compact looked cheap and shoddy. It would have meant nothing to her to know how many hours he spent searching Barntree to find something to please her; how hard put to it he was to raise the three pounds that it had cost him. For appearances' sake, she had been forced to admire it profusely when they had all opened their gifts after breakfast. She had sensed rather than seen Pierre's eyes watching her as she thanked Dick, knowing all the time he was laughing at her.

Publicly, Pierre's gift to her had been a pair of nylon stockings identical with those he had presented to Lady Allerton, Mercia and Tamily. The bracelet had been a pleasant surprise and now it was almost a comfort. It did at least prove that Pierre wanted something from her.

They had reached Allerton Manor now and Dick came hurrying out to open the car door for her. She gave him her secret smile.

'I was beginning to worry in case you'd had an accident. We've been home nearly an hour,' Dick told her, leading her into the warm hall. She felt the pressure of his hand on her arm and looked up into his clear, blue eyes.

He *was* attractive! In a few years time when Dick had ceased to be a boy, he would turn many more heads than Pierre could ever do. Sylvie had a flash vision of herself standing here beside Dick to receive their guests; 'Good evening, Lady Allerton; so good of you to have invited us to your beautiful home...' Yes, Dick would look very much the Lord-of-the-Manor when maturity added some lines to his clean young face; and she never doubted her own capacity to act the part of his wife. But would she be bored? Dick had told her his ambition was to farm part of the Allerton estate himself. She might bear the title she coveted, but there would be little joy in being a farmer's wife! Dick seemed to have no inclination for the smart Riviera life of casinos and lazy days idled away on sunwashed beaches. True, he had said he would like to visit her in New York but Sylvie suspected it was merely because he would be in her company. Somehow he did not seem to fit into the pattern of cocktail parties, night clubs and bars. He belonged to the out-of-doors and the last thing in the world she enjoyed was a good hearty walk.

Dick's favourite spaniel was snuffling around her expensive nylon stockings. She pushed the dog away with a gesture of barely-concealed dislike. The way these English let their dogs roam around their houses, muddying the beautiful, priceless rugs, leaving a trail of hairs on the rich brocade covers, drooling beneath one's chair at the dinner table! They treated their animals like human beings. It was repulsive.

She seemed suddenly to be seeing all the worst side of Allerton Manor and its occupants. The long Christmas dinner, followed course upon course in what she took to be English traditional manner; there was far to much to eat and everybody ate far too much of it.

The behaviour of Dick, Mercia, Tamily and Keith Parker—the latter at least might have tried to conduct himself with some decorum—seemed to Sylvie to be chidlish in the extreme. They clapped when the Christmas pudding, flaming with brandy was carried in on a silver platter by Simmonds; they pulled crackers; they wore the absurd paper hats on their heads and laughed uproariously over the mottoes. Even Lady Allerton was shrieking with laughter in a way Sylvie thought quite unfit for someone in her position. Lord Allerton looked on approvingly, carving the turkey and dispensing drinks and cigars, and wearing a ridiculous purple crown. No one was paying her much attention. They were all too busy enjoying themselves!

After dinner there was a brief lull over coffee. Then Lord Allerton retired to the library to sleep off his lunch; Lady Allerton went to her room and Mercia and Keith disappeared, presumably to the schoolroom to be alone.

Dick stretched his arms lazily above his head.

'The sun's still shining,' he remarked. 'Let's go down to the farm and have a look at Wendy's foal.'

Tamily leant forward, her eyes shining.

'I saw him yesterday morning, Dick. He's beautiful.'

She turned to Sylvie enthusiastically.

'He's only two days old and still wobbly at the knees. You *must* come and see him.'

Sylvie settled more comfortably into the deep winged chair. 'Nothing would persuade me to go for a·walk after a meal like that,' she said coolly. 'Why don't you two push off if you feel like it?'

Dick turned to her in dismay. 'But Sylvie, I wanted you to...'

He broke off suddenly and sharply aware that Sylvie couldn't care less what he wanted. His disappointment showed so clearly on his face that Tamily said quickly:

'I don't really want to go, Dick. Let's stay here and play Scrabble or something.'

He looked at her gratefully.

'I will come with you, Dick.' Pierre's accented voice startled them all.

Sylvie gave him a long, venomous look. She knew very well that Pierre had no interest in farms or livestock and that he disliked walking as much as she did. He could only have made such an offer to

113

curtail her plan to have a few hours alone with him.

Pierre was hardly the companion Dick had wanted, but his innate good manners made him rise from his seat instantly and to say:

'That's fine, Pierre. We'll leave the girls to be lazy together.'

Tamily remained seated, her whole body aching to get up and go out into the fresh air with Dick. She'd quite genuinely meant to go and see the foal again today but now she could hardly do so. She wondered what she and Sylvie could possibly have to say to each other. They had nothing in common. Nothing—except Dick.

Sylvie opened the conversation. 'And how do you like my friend, Pierre?' she questioned. 'He seems to have taken a great fancy to you.'

Tamily flushed.

'I—I think he's very nice.'

Sylvie blew out a cloud of smoke and stared across the room at the younger girl.

'Nice!' she repeated. 'This is a word you English use so often. I am never quite sure what it means. A view can be nice when you really mean beautiful. A pudding can be nice when you really mean tasty. A man can be nice when you might mean anything—a wonderfully uncompromising word, I think. What exactly did *you* mean by "nice", Tamily?'

Tamily sensed that Sylvie was trying to make her reveal herself. She said, stiffly:

'Perhaps I do not know myself what I meant.'

'Do you not find him attractive?' Sylvie asked, pointedly.

Tamily parried the question. 'Do you?'

She was surprised to see a swift, angry colour cloud Sylvie's pale complexion. Her question had been merely rhetoric. She had not considered Sylvie's feelings for anyone other than Dick. Now she knew that there was something between Sylvie and Pierre and wondered how the fact had escaped her before. Obviously, a woman like Sylvie did not go in for platonic friendships, not even if the men concerned were 'business contacts'. Yet if Pierre were Sylvie's lover, why had she invited him here for this holiday? It didn't make sense. If Sylvie were merely trying to make Dick jealous for the fun of it, she was playing a dangerous game. Pierre did not strike Tamily as being the kind of man who would willingly be made a fool of.

Obviously, if Sylvie were interested in Pierre, her excuse for inviting him as *vis-à-vis* to Tamily was nothing more than an excuse. Obviously Sylvie would not consider her as a rival for Pierre's attentions. Possibly it suited her to have two men dancing attendance.

'Poor Dick!' Tamily thought. His first love made him as gullible as she was herself. And this girl had brought neither of them anything but misery. With a spitefulness that was utterly foreign to her, Tamily probed deeper with the weapon Sylvie had given her.

'You must forgive me, Sylvie,' she said, 'I was mistakenly under the impression that you were in love with Dick. I would never have asked that question about Pierre if I had known you were in love with him.'

Sylvie tightened in her chair and said furiously:

'I never said...' she broke off and relaxed back in her chair, smiling enigmatically. 'You are more astute than I realized, Tamily. Since it interests you, I am a little in love with both of them. No doubt I shall make up my mind which I prefer in due course. It is interesting to have them here, side by side, to compare one with the other, don't you think? Such opposites—Pierre dark, mysterious, sophisticated, experienced; and Dick, young, deeply in love for the first time in his life, but oh, so innocent!'

Tamily looked at her companion in horror. That any woman could toy with the lives and feelings of two men with such cold-hearted disregard for the hurt she might inflict on them. It was horrible! And Dick loved her.

'Dick wouldn't love you if he knew what you were really like!' she cried impulsively. 'He'd despise you as much as I do.'

The older girl smiled. 'And who is to do the telling? You? Do you think he would listen to you? And even if he did, I should deny everything and say you acted from jealousy.'

Sylvie had meant 'jealousy of Pierre'. Seeing the hot, red colour burn in Tamily's face, for one moment she thought the girl might have fallen for Pierre after all. And then the truth flashed across her mind. Tamily was in love with Dick. It was no sisterly devotion she lavished upon him, as Dick supposed. It was a woman's love she had for him, jealous, possessive, protective, even in its hopelessness.

A kinder heart than Sylvie's might have felt a moment's pity for Tamily. But she felt mere amusement. This was something comical to her when she remembered some of Dick's comments about Tamily; 'She's a thoroughly good sort, Sylvie. You'll like her.' 'Tammy will approve of you, Sylvie—she always likes what I like.' 'Of course she's not really my sister, but we've grown up together and I feel the same way about Tam as I do about Mercia.'

'You can hardly accuse me of queering your pitch,' Sylvie said coolly. 'He's never been in love with you, has he? So why should you wish me harm?'

'Because you aren't good enough for him,' Tamily cried. 'You may be beautiful to look at but you're ugly inside. You have nothing to offer him, nothing. Why don't you go away and leave him alone? Can't you see how miserable you're making him? You don't really want him at all, you don't love him.'

'Perhaps not!' Sylvie agreed, sweetly. 'But he *is* attractive, Tamily. You will appreciate that. And besides, he'll one day have his father's title, won't he?'

Tamily was on her feet and about to

leave the room when she paused, suddenly struck by the thought that here was a way to get rid of Sylvie. It would be a terrible lie, of course, but it wouldn't be the first time she had lied to help Dick and she wouldn't be acting from jealous motives. Dick could never want her if he knew what she was really like.

Suddenly resolved, she turned her head and looked directly at the girl on the far side of the room.

'You are mistaken, I'm afraid, Sylvie,' she said quietly. 'Lord Allerton is a life peer only, and in case you don't know what that means, the title ends at his death. That means you can never hope to become Lady Allerton, can you?'

And turning on her heel, she went softly out through the door.

EIGHT

Keith had been on duty on Boxing Day but he came up after tea to see Mercia. As usual, they disappeared to the schoolroom. Although they had determined to keep the secret of their love for one another, their faces were so transparent that everyone in the household had guessed and Keith had had a word in private with Lord Allerton on Christmas Eve.

'You don't want an official engagement?' Mercia's father had asked, surprised.

'I don't think it would be quite fair to Mercia, sir,' Keith had replied. 'She's so young, isn't she?'

Lord Allerton had been impressed by Keith's thoughtfulness and although he wasn't quite the kind of husband he had had at the back of his mind for his only daughter, his liking for the young man overcame his disappointment that Keith had neither money nor position to offer her.

'I really wanted to let you know that my intentions were strictly honourable!' Keith had said, smiling. 'I seem to have spent so much time in your home lately. You must have been wondering about me.'

'M'wife did mention something about it!' Lord Allerton admitted. 'Well, nice of you to tell me. Haven't any objections m'self. Mercia's delicate, y'know—always has been. Not such a bad idea marrying a doctor, what?'

They'd had a drink together and it had been tacitly understood that Keith would be welcome whenever he could come along.

'I like your father!' Keith said, putting his arms round his young fiancée and holding her close. 'I wish my own father were alive—mother too. I know they would both have loved you, darling!'

His parents had been killed in the war in a bombing raid. His father, a doctor with a large practice in Inverness, had been on a fleeting visit with his wife to a colleague in London—their one and only visit to England during the war years. It had seemed all the more tragic, therefore, that they should have lost their lives for otherwise, the war had not really come near them. Fortunately, there was enough money for Keith to finish his medical studies and he now had a small income from his father's investments. Not really enough with which to support a wife who had been used to every luxury and comfort.

Keith sighed. It was only a few days since he and Mercia had agreed that they wouldn't marry for years to come. At the same time, he'd believed the waiting wouldn't be so hard. His joy that she really loved him sufficed in those first precious hours alone together. But now he felt himself under a growing strain. She was, in her complete innocence, so provocative. Unclouded by coquetry, she would be her adoring sweet self, clinging to him, prolonging their kisses and embraces, quite unaware of the strain on his emotions.

Her shyness, at first so marked, seemed to have vanished completely.

But he had underestimated Mercia's emotions. Her fragile appearance and delicate physique belied the strength of feeling of which she was capable. Hitherto, her affections had been lavished on those around her but because the very nature of her childhood illness had kept her apart, she was often alone and lived in a world of dreams beyond the immediate safe circle of her family. Romantic and idealistic, she had sat with a book on her lap, staring at a sunset or into the fire, thinking of the handsome young prince who would one day come to claim her. Sometimes this idol looked like Dick, sometimes like a youthful edition of her father. But always, he was kind, good, loving and needing her.

Now, suddenly, Keith had come. He

wasn't in the least like Dick or Lord Allerton but she had known right away who he was—the Prince of her dreams. At first, she had been afraid—afraid in case reality did not measure up to her ideals. But every hour spent with Keith had proved him to be all her heart desired. Her mind now at rest, she acted without inhibition or fear. Keith's tender love-making did not frighten her—indeed, it roused in her strange longings she tried to subdue. But since she would never deceive him, she did not try to hide them from him.

'Keith,' she said suddenly, and with impulsive sweetness, 'I don't think I want to wait years and years before we get married. I want to be with you now, all the time. I don't mind if we're poor. I want to be beside you, sharing your thoughts, and taking care of you. I used to be so happy here in this house, but now when you leave me I feel lonely and apart from it all. It's as if my heart goes with you. Please, Keith, couldn't we be married soon?'

It was so much what he, himself, desired, that for once in his young life, common-sense did not prevail. In any event, there was no real barrier against their marriage. He had believed Mercia to be too young, too immature, perhaps not sufficiently certain of her feelings for him. But this was no longer true; she was like a young girl dedicated, completely single-minded, in her love for him.

He held her very close, and with deep tenderness stroked the shining crown of her head.

'If your parents are willing, dearest, and you are quite, quite sure...'

'Yes, I'm sure!'

Quite suddenly she shivered in his arms. She felt a strange foreboding—almost as if this happiness could not last and she must reach out and hold it, bind it to her, before the dream vanished.

'I'm afraid, Keith,' she cried, in a small, frightened voice. 'Afraid of losing you. I couldn't bear it if anything were to part us.'

He lifted her into his arms and carried her like a child to the worn, chintz, nursery sofa.

'Whatever can be the matter with you, my darling?' he questioned, anxiously. 'What could possibly part us? Surely you don't believe that I could ever look at another woman now? You trust me, don't you?'

She stirred in his embrace, smiling uncertainly.

'I expect I was just being silly, Keith. But for the moment I felt frightened. I don't know what is the matter with me. Maybe it is just one of the symptoms of falling in love.'

'I can't confirm or deny that,' Keith said lightly. 'I've never been in love before. I wish there were more I could give you, Mercia. I wonder if you fully understand what it will mean to be married to a struggling young doctor? I wouldn't blame your father if he refuses his consent.'

'He won't, I'm sure he won't!' Mercia cried. 'I know all he asks is that I should be happy. I expect he will offer to help us, Keith. If he does, do you wish me to refuse?'

The young man considered her question thoughtfully. His natural Scots pride forbade him accepting help from anyone, perhaps more especially a future father-in-law. So far in life he had made his own way and he could proudly claim that he need thank no one but himself. But for once his price did not take first place. His love for this beautiful delicate, young girl was uppermost in his heart and mind and he knew that he would so anything, even lose a little of independence, if it meant her happiness.

'I want you to have exactly what *you* want,' he said gently. 'That is the only thing that matters to me.'

Mercia clapped her hands in childlike pleasure. Her usually pale cheeks were flushed with happiness and excitement.

'You're so wonderful to me, darling,' she cried. 'Let's go and ask Daddy's permission now, this minute.'

Keith looked at her thoughtfully. This impatience of Mercia's was so unlike her. Normally, she was a quiet, thoughtful, rather dreamy young girl, with a faraway look in her eyes, as if she were never quite following the conversation—a day dreamer. One could not conceive of such a person deciding on the spur of the moment on a course of action. It would have been more in keeping with her character to have dreamed over the idea for a long while, coming slowly to an eventual decision.

But her impatience charmed and delighted him, even while it surprised him.

Perhaps all women in love change a

little, he thought. After all, he too had deviated from his customary behaviour. He, too, liked time to consider a course of action, especially so momentous a one as this. He was fully aware of the enormous responsibility of marriage, particularly to a very young girl from a sheltered home and one who must always be physically delicate. Yet somehow, she had imparted to him that moment of fear, as if they must reach out and grab their joy in one another while it was still within their grasp.

He stood up and holding her hand tightly in his own allowed her to precede him down the long winding stairway to Lord Allerton's study.

In the drawing-room Dick stood by the french window staring out across the leafless winter landscape. A light drizzle blew across the empty flower-beds, and the wind soughed softly against the window panes. Yesterday's sunshine had gone, like Sylvie, and the desolation of the view struck an answering chord in his heart.

Behind him Tamily sat with her arms round her hunched knees, in front of the blazing fire. She sensed his misery and suffering. She alone knew that it was her fault—her lie—that had thrown Sylvie into Pierre's waiting arms.

Sylvie's slanting, continental handwriting sprawled across the note that lay crushed in Dick's clenched fist. Neither she nor Pierre had had the good manners to announce their sudden departure in person. They had slipped away quietly some time during the afternoon, while Tamily and Dick were looking at Wendy's foal. They had returned happily and enthusiastically to tea.

Simmonds had brought in Sylvie's note on the silver tea-tray and handed it to Dick without any expression on his impassive face, although he must have had a very good idea as to what it contained. Tamily knew very well that there was little went on in this house unremarked by the old family retainer. The family were far more than just people for whom Simmonds worked. They were *his* family and a lifetime of service to them had only increased his love for them all, with the possible exception of Lady Allerton. To the children, he was far more than a butler, he was their friend. And it was Simmonds' private opinion that Master Dick was very well rid of the young lady.

Dick turned from the window and paced the long room restlessly. Once he stopped automatically to take a sandwich from the tea-tray, and then threw it into the fire.

'*Why*, Tam?' he said, suddenly breaking the silence. 'That's what I don't understand. What made her rush off like that without a word? It doesn't make sense.'

Miserably, Tamily jabbed at the palm of her hand with a match-stick, watching the skin whiten where it was indented, and then swell gently out again and regain its colour.

'Don't do that, Tammy!' Dick said irritably. 'It's almost as annoying as your habit of twisting your hair round your finger when you're thinking. Sylvie didn't say anything to you, did she?' he went off at a tangent. 'Yesterday afternoon you were together. Dash it, Tam, you must have some idea—after all, you're supposed to be a woman—can't *you* understand? I'm damn'd if I can.'

Tamily bit deep into her underlip and looked up at him with sudden resolve.

'I think she went because she wasn't the least little bit in love with you, Dick. It wasn't you she wanted—it was your title. I think of the two of you, she probably came nearer to being in love with Pierre. She went to his room last night...' She broke off, finding it horribly difficult to meet the look on Dick's face, a look that combined unbelief, belief, and a desperate anxiety to go on hoping.

'I think you'd better go on, Tam,' he said quietly. 'You can't leave it there. What were you doing; spying on her?'

Perhaps he'd meant to hurt her. Perhaps she deserved it. She bent her head and looked down once more at her hands.

'No, I wasn't spying. I heard someone in the corridor and I thought it was Mercia. She had told me she hadn't been sleeping very well and I thought there might be something I could get for her. Sylvie didn't see me. She was just going into Pierre's room as I opened the door. I tried to go back to sleep. I swear I did, Dick, but somehow it just wasn't possible. It was daylight before I heard her close her own door. I'm sorry, Dick...'

He looked down at her, unwilling to accept her pity and angry with her for daring to commiserate with him.

'What the devil have you got to be sorry about?' he all but shouted at her. 'It wasn't *your* fault.'

'But it was, it was!'

She was weeping now, the tears rolling silently down her cheeks and dripping off the end of her nose. She caught each one with the tip of her tongue until they ran too fast and she was forced to brush them away with the back of her hand. Dick gave a manly sigh of exasperation, but his voice was more gentle as he said:

'Oh, for heaven's sake, Tam—take this!' He threw a clean handkerchief into her lap. 'And don't *sniff*, blow!'

He gave her time to obey him and then squatted down beside her.

'Now let's have it,' he said. 'I want the truth, Tamily.'

She told him in a small, choked little voice. He listened in silence and then to her utter amazement he gave his old cheerful laugh.

'You know, Tammy, one must admit it's got its funny side,' he said. 'I thought she was the most wonderful woman in the world. I wanted to marry her. I really loved her. I'd have given her anything in the world within my power to give, and I truly believed she was fond of me. What a young fool I've been! Don't cry over me, Tammy. I've regained my sanity. I can see

I'm jolly well out of it.'

He ruffled his hand over her dark curls and jumped to his feet, pulling her up beside him.

'I'm hungry,' he said, 'and I'll bet you are, too, Tam. Let's see what Simmonds has brought in for us.'

Tamily drew a deep, tremulous sigh. It was so hard to know if this was Dick putting a brave front on it or a Dick who had really recovered in a matter of minutes from his broken heart! Perhaps, she thought, it was a combination of both.

'Good,' Dick was saying, 'Sardine and tomato!'

He gave her a happy smile and a plate, and seemed not to have a care in the world.

NINE

Tamily knew she had no right to hope. Sylvie's departure had been a good thing for Dick but it did not alter the position between Dick and herself.

Ever since Sylvie's sudden disappearance on Boxing Day, Dick had sought Tamily out, demanding her time, her attention, her company. It was as if her presence somehow consoled him for the loss of his first love.

Tamily did not think that Dick's heart was broken. At times he was gay, cheerful, amusing and good fun to be with. But at other times she would find him unusually quiet and thoughtful, a hurt, puzzled look in his eyes, and she knew that he was thinking of the absent Sylvie.

There had been no word from her, no letter of explanation, not even a belated bread-and-butter 'thank-you' to Lord and Lady Allerton. The night Sylvie had left Lady Allerton had cross-questioned her son until he had left the room abruptly, saying:

'For God's sake, Mother. I don't know the reason any better than you do.'

Tamily had tried to explain. Her relationship with Lady Allerton had never been very close, but she did her best to make Dick's mother understand that Sylvie's casual behaviour had hurt Dick and that it might be best not to talk about it.

Fortunately, Mercia's sudden engagement to Keith and the announcement that they were going to get married at Easter had given Lady Allerton plenty to think and talk about, and Sylvie was soon forgotten. Lady Allerton's conversation was now concentrated on the trousseau, the list of wedding guests and preparations for an event she was determined to make into a big social occasion.

Mercia and Keith would have preferred a quiet wedding. But always unselfish, Mercia knew what pleasure it would give her mother to have a grand wedding with all the conventional trimmings, and for her sake was willing for Lady Allerton to 'have her head'.

'It doesn't really matter very much,' she told Tamily. 'The only thing I mind is that Keith and I should be married and I am so grateful that Mother and Father have given their consent. Keith and I were afraid they might think I was too young.'

Tamily wondered how much the sight of the two young lovers, the talk of weddings, and brides, added salt to Dick's wounded pride. Outwardly, he gave no sign of being affected. His manner towards Mercia was as gentle and kindly as it had ever been.

He seemed to be genuinely pleased at her happiness and to find much to like in his prospective brother-in-law.

Tamily doubted that anyone but herself guessed how deeply Sylvie had managed to hurt him. Sensitive as always to Dick's feelings, she had thought his laugh a little too loud, his search for something gay and amusing to do a little too enthusiastic, his occasional references to the beautiful Sylvie a little too casual.

But selfishly, she had welcomed his demands upon her, his need of her. He did not tease her quite so often and frequently they would have long, serious conversations about life, his future. She saw a new Dick. It was as if a little of the boyishness had died and a more serious, adult Dick was emerging.

He spoke a great deal of his plans to farm part of Allerton when he came down from Oxford.

'I'm not really interested in History,' he confessed, 'and I've no ambition to go on the Stock Exchange or become a big business wallah, or follow Dad into politics. I hear these other chaps talking about their careers and I've wondered if there's something odd about me, Tamily.

The only thing that seems a hundred per cent worth while is Nature. There's something lasting and immensely satisfying about the thought that when you plant a tree, it will still be growing hundreds of years after you're dead; that the woods will still be full of primroses and bluebells every spring; that the stream will still be flowing through ten-acre paddock when you and I are forgotten. One chap I said this to thought I was being morbid. He seemed to think such an idea depressing. But I find it exalting. It puts humanity, with its petty troubles and wars, and mad searching after money or position, into a proper perspective. People are little, transient creatures, put here to serve the Goddess of Nature. Man is only necessary, when you come to think of it, to till the ground and raise crops and rear livestock.'

Tamily had tried to follow his argument, sensing with love and understanding what he was trying to say.

'I don't altogether agree, Dick. After all, man only does those things to produce food to keep other men alive and procreate man. Nature could survive without his aid. He must, therefore, be here for some greater purpose.'

'Oh, no doubt God has His reasons for putting man on earth,' was Dick's casual reply, surprising her a little, for Dick's interest in religious questions had never been very marked.

'Have you spoken to your father about wishing to farm?' Tamily asked.

Dick shook his head. 'Not yet. I think Dad's rather keen I should take up politics, but I don't think he'll object when he gets used to the idea that I would make a better farmer than a politician. He's always loved the country.' He had linked his arm in hers. 'You know, Tam, you'd make a good farmer's wife. I was watching you with the lamb yesterday. You seem to have a private understanding with animals. They're never afraid of you.'

She had been unable to speak, her heart too full of wishful thinking. She could not envisage a happier or more contented life than the one he pictured so casually. If it could only... Oh, when would her disobedient heart recognize that there could be no future for her with Dick?

'Come to think of it, we'd make rather a good pair,' Dick said. 'We seem to think the same way about most things. What about coming into partnership with me, Tam?'

He turned to her with enthusiasm as the idea grew in his mind.

'You don't want to mess about as Mother's secretary. Mercia'll be getting married soon and you'll be bored to tears in this house. Now if Father would give me Lower Beeches, I'd get a really good dairy herd together. I'd have to go away to sales, so we'd need a man to run the place but you would be organizing things when I was away. We might have a small stud farm, too. In a couple of years' time, Wendy could have another foal, and you could raise a flock of turkeys. Of course, it's really better to specialize—you never make any money with mixed farms these days, but then we're not particularly interested in making money—that's the joy of it. We can have what we want, and blow the consequences!'

Once again, he was including her in his plans, taking her acceptance for granted. It wasn't fair to feel resentful, for he was perfectly right—she was happy no matter what he wanted her to share with him. But she wasn't sure if he really meant all this seriously, and if he did, whether she could bear the kind of platonic association he envisaged. Would she in time teach herself to put back the clock and see Dick only as an adored elder brother? Could she trust her heart not to betray her with some unguarded word or look?

'What about it, Tam? I certainly shan't get married now...' he paused, his eyes with that faraway look which she knew meant 'Sylvie'...'and you aren't the sort to fall madly in love like Mercia. We could have loads of fun, and the kind of life we both want. We've always been such good friends, we'd be bound to see eye-to-eye over the running of the place. We'd share the profits, of course, and then you could be independent. You wouldn't miss the allowance Mother gives you. Well, Tammy, what do you say?'

For a moment she hesitated. Dick didn't know it of course, but he was quite right in assuming she wasn't going to fall madly in love. Marriage with anyone else but Dick was so completely and utterly out of the question. This proposed partnership, if Dick were really serious, was more than she ever dared hope for. At least she would be near him, working with him, for him. In his own way, he loved her. It wasn't the way her heart craved, but surely that physical side to marriage was not the most important part. In a way, this partnership would be a kind of marriage, a sharing of their lives, a joint ideal, companionship, consideration for each other's wishes. Perhaps it would be possible for them to live at Lower Beeches. It seemed the whole world looked upon her as Dick's sister; was there any reason, therefore, why she couldn't keep house for him?

'It's a nice idea,' she said, with forced lightness. 'But you've got another two years at Oxford first, so it's early days to be planning. If you still want me to go into partnership with you when you come down, Dick, I think I'd enjoy it.'

Dick gave her a quick, friendly hug.

'You're a good sport, Tammy. You've always been a damn'd good sister to me. That day you told me about Sylvie—lying about the title, I mean, I reckoned you'd played a pretty dirty trick on me. But I ought to have known better. You're incapable of a mean thought. I want you to know that I know you acted for my good. I'm well rid of her and since it had to break up anyway, you were quite right in thinking the sooner the better.' He frowned, thoughtfully. 'I suppose it must seem mad to you when I say I still want her. I don't mean I'd marry her if she suddenly came back. I know she is a shallow, mercenary little bitch. But she's so damn'd beautiful, I can't seem to stop thinking of her. She had the most incredible way of looking at a chap. It made you want to make violent love to her. I think she knew just how provocative she was. I think she was deliberately trying to drive me round the bend. She knew just how much I wanted her and I think, that way, she wanted me too.'

It was as if he were talking to himself and then suddenly remembered that she was here. He gave her a shamefaced grin.

'I suppose I ought not to be talking to you like this. The funny thing is, Tammy, I forget you're a woman. When we're on our own like this it's like being with Philip—you know, the friend I told you about who shares my rooms. He's rather like you, what I call a listener. He lets me jaw away for hours and seems to understand what I'm getting at. I think you'd like him, Tam. Which reminds me, I've promised him I'll bring you up for

"Commem". I suppose now Sylvie's gone I shall have to find myself another girl. Perhaps Phil will invite his sister. He told me all about her one evening, but I wasn't paying much attention—mind too full of Sylvie, I suppose. Still, if she's anything like Phil, she'll be all right.'

If only she could armour herself against the stab of pain such remarks inevitably caused her. Perhaps she should be flattered that Dick looked on her as he might a good man friend. In a way it was a compliment, but why couldn't he see her as a woman? Why did he have to invite this other girl for May Week, and not her? Couldn't he see that she hadn't the slightest desire to meet Philip or any other man?

Fool, *fool!* she told herself for the hundredth time. It was better this way. What use would be served by Dick loving her? They could never be married.

Was it possible that Dick had thought of this and put her out of his mind? Jess had sworn that nobody knew the secret of her origin and there could have been no reason for Lady Allerton to disclose it since Dick had never displayed the slightest interest in her history prior to arrival at Allerton Manor. She pushed the idea away, knowing in her heart that she was and would always be no more than sister to him. She *must* be content with that. No doubt there were hundreds of girls far less lucky than she; girls who loved as deeply and as hopelessly and who had no part at all in the lives of the men they adored. There was the tragedy of her own mother's life. Jess must have loved Tamily's father just as deeply, just as completely, as she loved Dick; and how short-lived had been her few precious hours with him. She ought to be glad of the one relationship that was possible for them. Glad that at least the brotherly affection Dick had for her was deep-rooted and lasting, unless Tamily herself destroyed it. Nevertheless, when night time came and she lay alone in her room, despair would turn her thankfulness to torment, and the strain under which she was living gave way in a flood of hopeless tears.

It was pure chance that brought Mercia to her room late one night as she lay weeping. Mercia had been unable to sleep, either, her mind over-stimulated by the excitement of the day's events. Lord Allerton had called her and Keith to the library and informed them that he was giving them the Dower House.

'Your mother and I won't be ready to leave this house for a long time to come,' he told them kindly, 'and now there's no prospect of Dick making a youthful marriage it seems a pity to leave it empty. You'd better go on down and have a look at it and see if it will suit you.'

It was everything they wanted. The right size, with a room for a surgery if Keith were able to branch out on his own, a pleasant garden, and all within walking distance of Allerton Manor and Mercia's family. They had gone from room to room, planning, measuring, like two excited schoolchildren. And Mercia had become over-tired, over whelmed.

Usually the mild sleeping pills Dr Timms had prescribed for the occasions when she had one of her backaches or headaches were kept in her own bathroom. But she knew that Tamily had not been sleeping well, either, and guessed that she had possibly borrowed them since she could not find them on the shelf.

Mercia was appalled to see her dearest friend crying as if her heart were breaking. She was so happy herself, Tamily's tears were all the more shocking. She ran to the bed and flung her arms impulsively round Tamily's shaking shoulders.

'Tamily, darling, don't,' she whispered, anxiously. 'I can't bear to hear you crying—you of all people! Tell me what it is, please, Tamily.'

Tamily tried hard to regain control of herself. The last thing in the world she had wanted to do was to worry Mercia at such a time. If only she could think of some reason for her tears, other than the truth.

'I'm just—just tired!' she said, in a small, choked voice.

Mercia sat down on the bed and gently stroked the dark curls from Tamily's forehead.

'It's more than that, Tamily. Don't lie to me. Something's wrong, and you've got to tell me what it is. Have you forgotten our pact? I know we were only small when we promised always to tell each other everything, but I kept my side of it always. And I've trusted you to do the same.'

Tamily moved abruptly away from Mercia's comforting arms and walked across the room to the window.

'I can't tell you, I can't!' the words were wrung from her.

145

'It's Dick,' Mercia thought immediately. 'But why should she be distressed now? Sylvie's gone and Dick has been spending all his spare time with Tamily. Were Keith and I wrong to imagine that Dick was at last turning to Tammy on the rebound?'

'Perhaps I wasn't telling the truth just now,' she said quietly. 'I said I'd no secrets from you, but I have. I never told you that I guessed you were in love with Dick.'

Tamily swung round with an involuntary cry. The bright flush from crying still stained her cheeks but beneath it she was chalk-white with the shock of Mercia's admission.

'You know?'

Mercia drew in her breath. 'Tamily, don't look like that,' she said cheerfully. 'Of course I know. I've known for ages. I felt sure you would tell me when you were ready to do so, and so I didn't like to speak before. I guessed, you see, that Dick didn't return your love and that naturally your pride would forbid your accepting sympathy. But I'd hoped it was going to be all right. Especially when Sylvie departed. I believed Dick would come to his senses and fall in love with you. You've been together so much lately and

I know Dick's terribly fond of you.'

'Fond!' Tamily cried the word, bitterly. 'Oh yes, Mercia, he's fond of me. He asked me today if I would consider tying my future up with his. He wants us to farm Lower Beeches together. But he isn't in love with me. He never has been. I'm just a sister to him.'

'But he will see you differently one day, Tamily. I *know* it,' Mercia cried. 'I know Dick, and I know how much he needs you, even if *he* doesn't. I think he is in love with you but that he isn't aware of that fact.'

Tamily covered her face with her hands.

'Don't!' she whispered, 'Don't go on, Mercia. Even if Dick *were* in love with me we could never be married.'

It was Mercia's turn to look shocked. 'But why? Why?' she repeated.

The harsh words fell beyond control from Tamily's lips. 'Because I'm illegitimate.'

'But Tamily...!' Mercia broke off, uncertainly, and then began again: 'Even if it is true, nobody knows! And even if they did know, what difference would it make? It wasn't your fault. Nobody could blame you. Do you think it would affect my love for Keith if I were told now, this minute, that he were illegitimate? You're being fantastically old-fashioned.'

Tamily heard the words, and stared at Mercia uncertainly.

'But Mercia, Dick will one day be Lord Allerton. He'll have to make a good marriage. Even if Dick loved me enough not to mind, your mother, possibly your father, too, would never give their consent.'

Mercia considered the question. 'I don't see how either of them could possibly object,' she said at last. 'After all, Father didn't contract what you would term a "good marriage". Mother wasn't exactly illegitimate, but she came from the back row of the chorus and in those days was far less of a lady than your own mother.'

Tamily sat down in the armchair, so surprised that she was speechless. Lady Allerton a chorus-girl! It didn't seem possible. She was so very *grande dame,* so particular about etiquette, the conventions, so fastidious in her choice of those who were suitable society for her parties. No one ever came to Allerton Manor unless they had either money or position. At least she had always been perfectly open in her snobbishness.

She tried to put something of this into words. Mercia nodded in agreement.

'But that's exactly why!' she said. 'Mother was so afraid of doing the wrong thing that she'll lean over backwards to prove she can do the right. Look at my father, Tamily. He goes around in an antiquated pair of plus-fours, less well-turned out than some of his farm labourers, and he really does belong to one of the most aristocratic families in the country. Unlike Mother, he doesn't need to go around proving he's Lord of the Manor. I daresay Mother might in the circumstances raise a few objections. She has such high hopes for Dick and they're all part and parcel of her determination to run her family on the lines she thinks fitting for the aristocracy! But Father wouldn't mind—he's fond of you, too, Tamily, and Mother wouldn't be able to hold out for long against the rest of us.'

Mercia could see that her words had taken effect. Hope now shone in Tamily's eyes, though the tears still glistened. Sensitive, as always, to Tamily's wishes, she got up quietly and bidding her a soft good night left Tamily alone with her thoughts. She knew that *she* would sleep now, so glad was she to think that she had been able to bring Dick and Tamily a little closer together. It might be a long while before Dick woke up to the truth, but Mercia never doubted that in the end he must do so.

Tamily had no such conviction, but at long last she felt on equal terms with life. She could dare now, to hope.

TEN

Tamily stood in the church porch in the warm, spring sunshine, returning the smiles of the many village folk who were lining the path between the lych-gate and the church door, anxiously awaiting the arrival of the bride. Their faces were shining and excited, for this was no small wedding to them; it was their Squire's daughter who was being married today, and despite the modern shift of population in other parts of the country, here in this small rural area the inhabitants had for the most part remained unchanged. Many of them worked in one way or another on Lord Allerton's estate and had known Mercia since she was a tiny, golden-haired baby.

The bridegroom was generally approved of. In the short while since he had come to work with Dr Timms he had overcome their natural dislike of strangers and young and old spoke of the new doctor with liking and respect. What more fitting than that little Miss Mercia, who had always needed a great deal of care taken of her, should be marrying someone so well qualified to do so.

A light breeze stirred the tops of the yew trees but the sun was warm against the thin brocade of Tamily's bridesmaid's frock. It was a glorious shade of palest sky blue which Mercia had chosen with loving regard for Tamily's dark hair and eyes, and creamy skin. It was cut in traditional bridesmaid's style, with a heart-shaped neck, long tight sleeves, and a full, beautifully-draped skirt, which fell to the ground hiding the tiny blue satin sandals. For once, the dark-brown curls had been brushed carefully into the nape of her neck and over them was a wreath of apricot-coloured polyanthus roses. The same tiny, button-size flowers made up her Victorian posy, interspersed with palest blue hyacinth bells perfectly matching her dress.

'You look stunning!' had been Dick's comment before he had departed for the church to do his duty as usher. 'Not like yourself at all.' A back-handed compliment, perhaps, but one she hugged tightly to her with pleasure as she awaited Mercia's arrival with Lord Allerton.

The church behind her was packed with the family's guests, mostly friends of the Allertons; one of Keith's aunts had come the long journey from Scotland, and there were two or three doctors who had been students with him. Tamily had been aware of their glances in her direction, and despite the fact that she had eyes only for Dick, was feminine enough to be pleased with their admiration.

She felt wonderfully happy. It was such a beautiful day and Mercia, whom she had left only a few moments ago, was the most beautiful and angelic-looking bride Tamily had ever seen. She was a fairy-tale bride, all in white with her shining golden hair only half-hidden beneath the cascading delicate net veil that had been her great-grandmother's. 'Happy the bride the sun shines on.'

'And she will be happy! I know she will!' Tamily thought.

The old saying that the course of true love never ran smooth had truly been disproved in the case of Mercia and Keith. Theirs had been a perfect courtship, universally approved. There might not be much money but Lord Allerton's gift of the Dower House had solved one problem and the many elaborate wedding gifts that filled two rooms in the Manor would help to furnish their new home.

A ripple of movement went through the watching crowd and a voice cried:

'She's come. She's here!'

Lord Allerton's Rolls, an unrecognizable Benson in a new smart uniform at the wheel, pulled up at the old lych-gate. Benson hurried out and opened the door. Lord Allerton in morning suit, with a superb white carnation in his buttonhole, climbed out and held his arm ready for his daughter. Tamily was temporarily blinded by a series of flashes from the London photographers who had not until this moment let themselves be seen; Mercia hesitated momentarily and then climbed out of the car and took her father's arm.

The crowd gasped; admiring comments passing from one to the other in a long murmur of approval. Mercia looked pale but composed. She smiled briefly at Tamily, who took up her place behind her.

Someone had passed the word into the church, for suddenly the organ music swelled out with the Bridal March from *Lohengrin*. Slowly, Lord Allerton led his daughter out of the bright sunshine and into the flower-decorated church. Tamily herself had arranged the flowers, vase after vase of fresh spring blooms. No lilies, no carnations, nothing exotic for someone as sweet and young as Mercia. Instead, Tamily had chosen white lilac, narcissi, hyacinths, Easter palm, and white iris. The only colour came from the vases of long-stemmed, pale pink roses that Mercia loved.

The beautiful smell of the flowers pervaded the church. On the altar the candles burned brightly and in front of them waited Keith and his best man, Dr Timms.

Unlike the usual bridegroom, Keith did not seem in the least nervous. He watched his bride come slowly up the aisle towards him, a faint smile of love and welcome on his handsome face. He took his place beside her and the age-old wedding service began.

Tamily was standing close behind Mercia, and level with the front left-hand pew where Dick now stood beside his mother. She was conscious of his deep voice joining in with the choir in the wedding hymn 'O Perfect Love'. She was too filled with emotion to sing herself. There was no room for sorrow today, only for joyous gladness and a rush of tenderness for the young bride.

Mercia's voice was surprisingly loud and clear when she answered the vicar's question:

'I will!'

A moment later they were kneeling in prayer and Tamily, hearing Dr Timms coughing huskily beside her, knew that he was as deeply moved by this ceremony as she was herself. The vicar's address was a short but happy one. It was as if he, too, realized that there was no need to forewarn this young couple about the dangers of marriage in modern days; as if he were fully aware of the deep, lasting quality of their love. His theme seemed to rest on the fact that these years of youth and loving would be the happiest of their lives and that they must treasure every moment as a gift from God.

Tamily saw Keith's hand reach out and clasp his bride's and for one tiny moment she felt her own apartness, aloneness. Then as the organist swept into the opening bars of the Trumpet Voluntary, Dick and his mother took their place behind her and they went forward into the vestry.

The register signed, Mercia turned to Tamily to receive her friend's congratulatory kiss.

'I'm so happy, Tammy!' she whispered, 'I wish I could be sure this wasn't a dream.'

Then her family came to her and Tamily busied herself collecting Mercia's beautiful bouquet of pink and white roses, took up her own posy and they were going back into the church, Keith proudly leading his unveiled bride on his arm. The sunshine poured through the open door to welcome them back once more and the guests crowded behind Tamily as she stood watching the first photographs being taken.

Presently, the white-ribboned wedding car drew up and under a hail of confetti, bride and groom departed.

Beside her, Tamily heard Dick's amused voice.

'And I wonder who'll get fined for this lot of litter!'

But there was no time to reply to him.

The second car had stopped at the lych-gate and Dick moved forward to open the door for his parents and Dr Timms.

'Your turn next, Master Dick!' called someone in the crowd. Dick turned, smiling, and called back:

'I won't be caught so easily, Ted.'

'Don't you be so sure, Master Dick. You'm a mighty fine catch for some lass.'

Dick closed the car door and walked back to old Ted. Ted had been head gardener at Allerton Manor for two generations and now, nearly ninety years old, he had somehow managed to get himself down to the church to see Mercia married. His age and erstwhile position in the family privileged him to speak his mind as he wished.

Dick looked at the gnarled old face with amusement. 'And who d'you think's going to catch me?' he asked.

Aware of his audience, Ted was not going to be out-witted. 'What about Miss Tamily there? She'm no relation of your'n, Master Dick. You'm couldn't find a prettier lass in the whole of Sussex.'

Dick turned to look at Tamily, his eyes twinkling with laughter. He saw with surprise that she was blushing and then the onrush of guests leaving the church put an end to the conversation, and Tamily hastily made her way to the waiting car.

As she was driven the short distance to the Manor, her mind whirled. She felt she would never be able to look Dick in the face again. If only she hadn't blushed! If only she could have laughed, as Dick had done, as if it were all a mighty fine joke. Of course, Old Ted had been teasing—he couldn't have known how she felt. The villagers might credit him with second sight, but she knew better.

It was Ted's custom to sit on the oak bench outside the village pub, his head nodding, pretending to be asleep; when all the time his sharp old ears were listening to what went on around him. His shrewd guesses as to the outcome of what he heard had given him his reputation. She had often stopped to chat with him on her way to buy sweets at the village shop and she knew he was fond of her. He would never have willingly embarrassed her, she was sure.

But she need not have worried. Dick seemed to have forgotten her blushes completely, if indeed he had ever noticed them, as he stood beside his family to receive their guests. The long line of people filed past and Tamily, suddenly weary, wondered how Mercia managed to stand so upright with a charming word and smile for each one of them.

'She must be tired,' Tamily thought anxiously. 'I'll tell Dick to see they get away as early as possible.'

But it was two hours before she went upstairs to help Mercia change into her going-away costume. There were now deep circles beneath Mercia's eyes, and she admitted her exhaustion quite readily.

'Don't worry, darling,' she said to Tamily. 'Keith will look after me. Oh, I'm so happy, so wonderfully happy.'

Tamily did as much as possible to help her, keeping the voluble Lady Allerton out of her daughter's room until the last possible moment; packing the last few things into the waiting suitcases; finding Mercia's gloves and bag, and then bringing Keith to the room to escort her downstairs. At the door, Mercia turned and went back to the bed where her bridal gown and bouquet lay. She took the beautiful bunch of pink and white roses and thrust them into Tamily's arms.

'Not just because it's the custom, darling,' she whispered, 'but because you're dearer to me than anyone else in the world, except Keith.'

Tamily didn't follow her down the stairs. There were plenty of people to see her off with shouts of good wishes and gay laughter. She stood still in Mercia's room, untidy now with crumpled tissue paper, discarded clothes, and half-opened drawers. The transient March sunshine had disappeared and the shadows were creeping across the carpet towards her. In the distance, she could hear Keith's car revving up, then the sound faded away. They were gone. 'The tumult and the shouting dies' Tamily thought, remembering her Kipling.

Deathly tired all at once, she bowed her head over the beautiful roses she still held in her arms, and knew that with Mercia's going she had lost not only her dearest friend, but her only ally. Soon Dick would be on his way back to Oxford and she would be the only one of the three left behind.

She had never felt more alone.

ELEVEN

Tamily lay on her bed in the Mitre Hotel. She had already spent one night here and found the old Tudor Coaching House both comfortable and an agreeable home-from-home in which to be spending these four days of 'Commem'. The old building with its beams and low ceilings and sloping, highly-polished floorboards, somehow seemed to fit into the character of this historic city.

Dick's friend, Phil, had been telling her how much Oxford had changed since the pre-war years. Apparently the setting up of industries on the outskirts of the city had brought the inevitable housing estates and with them had come the multiple stores and an ever-increasing population. But Tamily found the place fascinating. This afternoon, Phil had taken her on a walking tour, showing her many of the beautiful colleges, the Bodleian Library, and the Ashmolean; the High Street with its olde-worlde shops, unchanged over the centuries.

Phil undoubtedly had a great love of antiquity. No doubt part of it was due to the fact that his father was an archaeologist. His sister, too, had been caught up in the fascination of the past and was planning to join her father in an archaeological expedition to Cyrene. But Phil's main interest was modern history, and much to his father's disappointment he had no desire to go to Libya.

Tamily tried to shut off her thoughts. She had hoped to be able to manage a few hours sleep before the dance tonight. She had been up at five o'clock this morning, in time to go with Dick and Phil to hear the traditional May Morning anthems of the choirboys at Magdalen. Dick had been particularly anxious to go because this was his first 'Commem', too. It was Phil's second year but apparently he was determined as they were not to miss it.

There had been quite a gathering of people to hear the boys' voices ringing out with strange beauty across the sharp morning air. Tamily had been fascinated, and strangely moved. All three of them had eaten a large breakfast afterwards in a nearby coffee-house, opened especially early for the event. Afterwards, Dick had returned to his College for some lectures but Phil had cut his own in order to take Tamily round Oxford.

She liked Dick's friend immensely. He was Dick's opposite—quiet, thoughtful, unremarkable. He lacked Dick's easy, boyish charm and his conversation was stiled and spasmodic, no doubt due to shyness. But after an hour or two together, he had begun to converse more freely with her and Tamily knew that he liked her. She liked being with him. It was such a novelty to her to be 'taken care of'. Used as she was to Dick's casual behaviour, Phil's solicitude touched her with gratitude. He insisted upon lending her his overcoat because quite a chill breeze blew down the streets. He insisted they should stop for mid-morning coffee, telling her she must be tired with so much walking. Tamily was not used to considering her own welfare, and his repeated attention to the smallest detail of her comfort flattered and pleased her.

She liked, too, what she privately thought of as his 'india-rubber' face. She termed it thus because there were no straight lines—it was a mobile, fluid face, with a slightly lop-sided nose, rather wide-apart, unusually grey eyes, topped with an untidy

163

crown of light-brown hair. His eyes were very heavily fringed with dark lashes and were far too beautiful for the rest of his face. Nothing seemed quite to match; no feature would fit in with another. One would never have called him handsome, and yet he was not displeasing to look at.

She knew that Dick had invited her as a partner for Phil. Phil's sister, Anthea, was to have come as Dick's *vis-à-vis*. Unfortunately, Anthea had 'flu and it was too last-minute notice for Phil to find another girl. So Tamily would have two escorts tonight. No doubt she would be required to do a lot of dancing, and she knew she ought to sleep for a short spell, if she possibly could. But sleep eluded her. She was too stimulated by all the new impressions she had received.

Unlike most girls of her age, there had been very few occasions when she had been away from home except for family holidays. She had certainly never been away on her own, before. And were it not for Dick's insistent letters, she might not be here now. She had had no desire to come as *Phil's* partner.

Now, however, she was immensely glad to be here. She liked Phil, and Dick was in wonderfully good form. He seemed to have recovered completely from the unfortunate ending of the affair with Sylvie and, from what she could gather from Phil this afternoon, he had buckled down at last to some hard work. There had been no need for her to bring Dick's name into the conversation. Phil spoke of him often, with a combination of paternal interest and affection, and genuine respect.

'Chaps like me have to study like hell to make the grade,' he had told her with a rueful smile. 'Dick hardly puts pen to paper and only has to read through a book once to be able to master the contents. If he would only take his work more seriously, he'd have no trouble at all in walking away with all the honours. But he just doesn't seem to bother one way or another.'

'I expect that's because he is not intending to make use of his History Degree if he gets it,' Tamily had explained. 'He's only interested in farming.'

Phil had given her his deep, slow smile. 'You're telling me! I hear of little else but Lower Beeches and how you and he are going to run the place.'

'Me?' Tamily had echoed, involuntarily.

Phil had looked surprised. 'Why, yes. I gathered you were just as keen as Dick. You know, Tamily, you're not in the least like I expected. From Dick's description I'd rather imagined a red-cheeked country girl, plump, probably horsy. You frightened me to death when you stepped off the train looking like a *Vogue* model girl.'

Despite her chagrin at Dick's inadvertent description of her, Tamily had to smile.

'I must say, you did look a bit scared,' she agreed. 'But not more scared than I felt. It was fortunate for both of us that Dick did all the talking.'

'But you looked so poised and self-controlled,' Phil had argued. 'I find it hard to believe you were nervous.'

'Then I must have learned to cover up better than I thought,' Tamily said quietly.

She wondered how long it would be before Phil realized that she was in love with Dick. Or would he have assimilated Dick's view of her—that she was his 'kid-sister'. She knew she would have to make an effort tonight not to listen always to what Dick said, not to let her eyes follow him round the room, not to look too happy when he asked her to dance, or put an arm affectionately round her shoulders. She would give as much of her attention to Phil and maybe some miracle would happen and Dick could be jealous, wanting her for himself, seeing her at last through another man's eyes.

She wished she could be sure whether this new hopefulness was less painful than the days before Mercia had spoken to her and she had been without hope. Now she read and re-read every line of Dick's letter, searching for a word, a phrase, which might mean his attitude to her had changed. But his letters were, as always, casually affectionate—no different in any way from the ones he wrote to Mercia.

Somewhere deep down inside her, she had allowed herself to imagine that Dick would greet her at the station yesterday with a changed heart. Her mind had told her that there was no justification whatever and that she was mad to let her heart beat the way it did as the train drew near to Oxford, but her heart as always paid no attention to her mind and she had searched the rows of faces amongst the waiting group, hoping despite herself for Dick to run forward and put his arms around her.

She ought to have known better. Dick's hug was as devoid of a lover's meaning as was the kiss he planted on her forehead.

Her thoughts had made her restless once more, and Tamily gave up any idea of sleep. She glanced at the clock beside her bed and saw that it was half past six. She resolved to start dressing, giving herself plenty of time to take all the trouble she wished over her hair, her bath, her nails.

Surprisingly, she was only just ready when the bedside telephone rang with a message to say that Phil was already waiting downstairs. She tried to curb a momentary disappointment that Dick had not managed to be first. She took a last look at her reflection in the long mirror.

She had wanted to wear her blue brides-maid's dress, but Mercia had persuaded her into the extravagance of a new dance frock especially for the occasion, and had helped Tamily to choose it. It was a far more feminine dress than Tamily would have picked on her own. The white net skirt billowed from her small waist like a waterfall, caught here and there with tiny blue lovers' knots. The white brocade bodice was cut low over the bosom, revealing the gentle curve of her shoulders and arms and dipping at the back almost to her waist. Around her neck hung the gold locket which had been Keith's present to her as bridesmaid. It was empty when he had given it to her but now it contained a photograph of Dick as a child—a chubby baby, with a crop of golden curls over the same twinkling blue eyes. It was unmistakeably Dick, although he had been only three when the photograph was taken. She would never open it to show the contents to a living soul. Not even Merica knew what was inside. Tamily knew that it was silly to be so sentimental but this far at least she could indulge herself.

Despite the colour she had added to her cheeks, her face was pale and there were small shadows beneath the dark eyes. It was a sad, thoughtful face which stared back at her from the impersonal mirror and with an effort she tried to alter the expression. Tonight she would be gay—the gayest girl at the ball. With a little sigh she turned and went downstairs to the waiting Phil.

She would have had to be blind not to see the look that came into Phil's eyes as he stepped forward with his usual good manners to greet her as she came down the old staircase.

'You look beautiful, Tamily!' he said shyly, and she knew that he meant it. It was balm to the wound Dick's description had inflicted—'a red-cheeked, country girl, plump and probably horsy.' No doubt Dick hadn't used those exact words, but such had been Phil's impression of her, none the less.

Phil led her through to the lounge and settled her comfortably by the fire. 'It's a bit chilly, and I don't want you to catch cold!' he said solicitously.

With feminine intuition, she knew that she could make Phil fall in love with her. While he disappeared to the bar to fetch drinks for them, she toyed momentarily with the idea. How comforting it would be to have someone like Phil to adore her the way Keith adored Mercia. How pleasant to be able to sit back and relax, knowing you were adored. How soothing to her hurt pride to know that one man, at least, thought her worthy of love.

Then the thought cast instantly from her mind, as a tall, fair-haired young man came walking across the room towards her, smiling apologetically.

'I say, I hope I'm not late, Tammy. Been waiting long?'

He lowered himself into the chair beside her and stretched his long legs towards the fire.

'Phil turned up yet?'

'He's getting drinks,' Tamily said.

'Good fellow! I say, Tam, what d'you think of him? He's fallen for you in a big way.'

Tamily blushed, and noticing her heightened colour Dick grinned mischievously.

'Don't say you've fallen too?' he teased.

'Don't be silly, Dick,' she said more sharply than she had intended. 'We've only known each other a day.'

'Long enough, long enough!' Dick replied, undaunted. 'I thought you two would get along. You've knocked Phil all of a heap. He couldn't wait to get along here this evening, although I told him you'd probably still be sound asleep.'

He glanced down at her, and continued:

'I must say you're looking a bit of all right.' He used the cockney phrase deliberately. 'Positively blooming! Must be love, what?'

She couldn't stand his teasing. 'Shut up, Dick,' she said in a soft, furious undertone.

171

But Dick refused to be put off. 'Now, now, Tammy. Keep your hair on. I'm not going to spoil your evening, don't worry. I shall disappear discreetly at the appropriate moment.'

She could have wept. How could he be so blind.

Phil's return put an end to Dick's chaffing. If he noticed Tamily's sudden quietness he was too good-mannered to remark on it, and Tamily managed to recover her self-control before the three of them went in to dinner. The dining-room was crowded, mostly undergraduates with their girl friends, all in high spirits. Tamily tried to capture some of the bright, carefree atmosphere that surrounded her. Dick was on top of his form, regaling them with amusing anecdotes about his tutors and flirting quite shamelessly with a rather pretty fair girl at a neighbouring table.

'Wonder if she's going to the same dance?' he said aloud. 'Don't know the fellow she's with, do you, Phil?'

Tamily tried not to notice as the girl turned her head and looked across at Dick in the way that reminded her too poignantly of Sylvie. There was invitation and promise in that glance. Tamily realized, suddenly, that if this was what attracted Dick, she hadn't a chance. She didn't know how to go about this game of looks. There was nothing of the coquette in her make-up. She would never be able to play the game of catch-me-if-you-can. Her feelings were much too intense.

Tamily imagined that she must be different from other girls. She didn't realize that love, real love, had come into her life so early that the time of youthful flirtation had passed her by. Flirtation was for the beginning of love, the period when two young people were getting to know one another, attracted and yet not sure whether they wished the moment to go beyond that point.

That same fair-haired girl would be just as artless as Tamily when she really gave her heart, just as defenceless, just as direct. True love knows no deception, admits no pretence, and wishes only to give. Flirtation would be too shallow a vessel to contain it.

The dance itself was a crowded, noisy affair. Few people there could have been over twenty-five; only one or two of the dons with their wives. Tamily felt herself caught up in the uninhibited gaiety of youth. Dick whirled her round the crowded floor, bumping occasionally into other couples, laughing, apologizing, and dancing away again. Once or twice one of his friends would tap Dick on the arm and say: 'Give us a break, old boy. Just one dance.'

But Dick would shake his head and rush her off once more on the floor. He didn't even give Phil the chance to dance with her.

Tamily did not dare to stop and question this monopoly of her time. It was enough that he wanted her; that he wasn't prepared to relinquish her to anyone. She was wonderfully happy. The time flew by and with considerable surprise she heard Dick say: 'Good heavens, it's nearly midnight!'

Abruptly he led her from the dance floor, and seeming to know just where to find him, deposited her at Phil's side in the crowded bar.

'Well, old boy, here she is, safe and sound. Now I shall tactfully withdraw and remove my irksome presence.'

Without a backward glance he turned and walked away from her and was soon lost in the thronging crowd. Tamily stared after his retreating figure uncomprehendingly. Some of her shocked surprise must have shown on her face, because Phil said suddenly:

'We made a pact, Tamily. Dick would have the first half of the evening and I the second.'

She tried hard to digest this piece of information and not feel too much like a box of chocolates being shared equally between two schoolboys. If only one of them had told her what was happening; if only she could have prepared herself for Dick's abrupt departure...

Phil was looking at her thoughtfully.

'I'm sorry, Tamily. Perhaps we should have asked you... Do you mind? I mean...well, I could probably find Dick...' he broke off awkwardly.

Tamily lifted her head proudly and looked directly at him.

'I don't mind in the least,' she lied, coolly. 'In fact, I'm pleased it's this way round. I'd rather have the last half of the evening with you.'

Phil looked absurdly pleased by her comment. For one moment he had wondered if Tamily's interest in Dick was more than that of a sister. There had been something in her expression which had made him wonder...but of course, that was absurd. Dick had spoken so often of Tamily and made it absolutely plain that she was linked with his sister Mercia just as truly as if she had been his real sister.

He comforted himself with this thought as he danced slowly round the room, holding Tamily's slim young body in his arms. He knew that he'd fallen in love—something he'd believed would never happen to him. He didn't care for girls, not the bright young things whom the other chaps went into ecstasies about; nor the rather plain, serious-thinking 'blue stockings' that were his sister Anthea's friends. Least of all could he raise any enthusiasm for the flashy, heavily-made-up young women who hung around Oxford openly ogling the undergraduates and waiting to be picked up.

Tamily was different. She seemed to combine beauty with a lively, intelligent brain. There was something wistful and sad which roused in him a desire to protect her. He had realized during their afternoon together that she was something quite apart from other girls and that he'd been incredibly lucky to meet her. He hadn't dared to hope that she might find him attractive, too. He had lived too long with his frank, outspoken sister to have any illusions about himself. He knew he was awkward, shy and far from good-looking. He hadn't much to offer a girl and yet, miraculously, Tamily seemed to like him. He could hardly believe his good fortune.

At least an hour must have passed before he noticed suddenly how tired she looked. He could have gone on dancing with her all night, but sensing her fatigue he put his own desires aside.

'I'm going to take you back to the hotel,' he said at the end of the next dance.

Tamily made a half-hearted protest. He was so nice, so kind, it hardly seemed fair to cut short 'his half' of the evening. And yet she *was* tired, desperately so.

He ignored her protest and told her to go and find her cloak.

He wanted to get a hired car to drive her back but it was only ten minutes walk and Tamily said she would far rather walk the short way with him. Outside, the night sky was studded with stars and a brilliant three-quarter moon lit up the narrow, twisting streets which were now almost deserted. Phil took Tamily's hand and since she made no effort to withdraw it, held it tightly as they wandered along the High Street towards the hotel. Tamily tried not to wonder where Dick was—if he had found the little blonde girl from the dinner-table, or someone else with whom to walk home in the moonlight. In her loneliness of heart, the warm pressure of Phil's hand was immensely comforting. She wondered if he would try to kiss her before they reached the hotel; whether she would let him. Bitterly, she considered the fact that she was nearly eighteen and had never been kissed.

'Why not? Why not?' she thought, unhappily. 'Dick wouldn't care. There was nobody to care, and if it would make Phil happy...'

The moment came and she heard Phil's voice, low and husky, against her cheek as he drew her into his arms.

'You're so beautiful, Tamily!'

She gave herself hesitantly to his embrace. His mouth came down on hers with a warm, demanding kiss that asked something of her she felt unable to return. She closed her eyes and tried to think of nothing but Phil and the soft endearments he was speaking. If she could only lose herself in the comfort of his nearness; in the consolation of no longer being alone. But even while unconsciously her arms went round his neck, her mind held her apart, seeing herself with surprise in another man's arms. She broke away from him so abruptly that the man beside her felt sure he had offended her.

'I'm sorry, Tamily,' he apologized. 'I shouldn't have...'

'It's all right, Phil!' she broke in quickly. 'It's nothing you've done...I wanted you to kiss me...it's not your fault. I'm the one who should apologize.'

He stared at her in bewilderment. She seemed so upset and yet she had assured him that it was not anything he had said or done.

'What is it, Tamily? Can't you tell me?' he asked quietly. 'If something is wrong, I'd like to be able to put it right for you. I want you to be happy. I know this will sound crazy but I swear it isn't the moonlight, or "Commem" or anything silly like that, but I've fallen in love with you. I don't expect you to care for me in return. I don't want anything from you—only that you should be happy.'

This was unbearable, coming from the wrong person, words she had longed so desperately to hear from another man's lips. Tears burned her eyelids, and rolled down her cheeks unchecked. She was so tired, not just physically, tired from what now seemed to be an endlessly long day, but mentally exhausted from the emotional battle between her heart and her acceptance of the truth. Dick would never love her. If she could only bring herself to accept the fact, she might yet find some sort of consolation with a man like Phil.

She stood immobile, staring at him in the moonlight, unable to speak for the tears that were choking in her throat. Then he stepped forward and put his arms round her and she was crying against his shoulder. He stroked her hair gently, not understanding and yet strangely content that she had turned to him with her troubles. When she was ready she would tell him and he would help her. There must be some way he could help her.

'Here!' he pushed a clean white handkerchief into her hands and watched her scrub at her eyes like a small girl. 'The men will be ragging me if I go in with powder and lipstick all over my d.j. You know what, Tamily, I think a good hot cup of coffee would do you the world of good. There's an all-night café not far from here. What do you say?'

'I can't!' she said in a small, muffled voice. 'I must look a sight. I'm so sorry, Phil—to spoil your evening this way.'

'Who are you hoping to attract in a café at this time of night?' Phil teased her, gently. 'You look all right to me, and that's all that should matter.'

Tamily smiled through the last of her tears and obediently allowed Phil to recapture her hand and continue their walk down the quiet street.

'You're awfully nice, Phil,' she said warmly. 'I'm so glad you're Dick's friend.'

It was only then he realized that he had not been wrong after all. Tamily was in love—with Dick.

TWELVE

Two days went by before Tamily finally admitted the truth to Phil—two days spent almost solely in each others company. They had wandered through Christ Church Meadows, visited Phil's favourite haunts, danced, punted on the river in the bright May sunshine. Sometimes Dick had gone along, too, but more often than not Phil and Tamily had been alone. In a way, she had preferred the hours when Dick was not there. Without him the tension was eased and there was a strange, satisfying contentment in Phil's pleasant company.

He had not tried to kiss her again although sometimes he held her hand and she knew that he was very fond of her, if not in love with her. She wished desperately that she could fall in love with him. How simple and easy life would be if only her heart would obey her mind.

Phil was not handsome but he was so very nice, one ceased to think of him in terms of looks. Tamily knew he would make the perfect husband, reliable, dependable, kind, adoring. He spoilt her even now. If she professed a preference for a particular brand of chocolates, he would bring them with him the next time they met; if she admired one particular stretch of the river, he would make a point of going there a second time. He already knew that she preferred tomato juice to cocktails before lunch, and sherry before dinner at night.

He knew the names of her favourite tunes, her favourite flower, the books she liked. He was always asking her questions about herself and never tired of listening once he had persuaded her to talk.

Now, after two days, she was as much at home and at ease in his company as if she had known him all her life. It was her last day at Oxford. Tomorrow she would return to Allerton Manor and the old life which now seemed almost another world. She had meant to return yesterday. But Phil had persuaded her to prolong her visit another twenty-four hours. Because it mattered so much to him, she agreed and was glad now she had done so. The May sunshine was really warm as it blazed down on their bare heads. Phil had tied the punt up to a leaning willow and they were stretched out side by side, enjoying the warmth on their faces. Suddenly, irrelevantly, for they had been discussing books until then, Phil said:

'You know I was telling the truth when I said I'm in love with you, Tamily?'

She lay perfectly still, not yet sure of what she must say to him in reply. This was no casual remark, no brief flirtation.

She knew that. Phil was deadly serious and she must not hurt him.

He leaned over on his side, watching the changing emotions showing on her transparent face.

'Don't be sorry!' he said. 'I know you aren't in love with me.'

'Is it—so obvious?' The words were a cry full of bitterness which hurt him for her sake.

'No! I don't think I'd have been sure if it weren't for loving you. I can feel you *like* me—and that's as far as it goes.'

'Oh, Phil!' She turned her head then so she could look into his eyes. 'It's more than just liking. I'm very fond of you. I'd *like* to be able to fall in love with you. I...I just can't!'

'Darling!' The endearment slipped from him. 'No one can make themselves fall in love. There's someone else, isn't there?'

She nodded mutely.

'Tell me!'

He had a right to know—to know the truth.

'It's Dick. I suppose that shocks you. Everyone seems to take it for granted we're kind of adoptive brother and sister. But I don't feel sisterly towards him,

Phil. I think I've always loved him, ever since I was a little girl. I wish I could stop.'

'I guessed as much,' Phil admitted. 'It seems a cruel trick of fate to have thrown you both together when you were kids. If you'd grown up apart—suppose I'd invited you up for Commem as my girl, Dick would have seen you as you really are. He must be blind, Tamily. And it's so unlike Dick. He always has an eye for the beautiful ones—yet he can't seem to see you.'

Tamily smiled ruefully.

'He sees me, but not as a woman!' she said. 'It's no use, Phil. I know it's no good. Dick will fall in love with someone one day and then I shall know it is all over. I try not to hope. Deep inside me, I *know* there isn't a hope. It's all so silly, isn't it?'

'Not silly—tragic!' Phil said warmly. 'Surely something can be done. Let me talk to him. I could make him...'

'No!' Tamily cried sharply. 'You just said yourself that people can't be made to fall in love. Dick would be terribly embarrassed. He'd be upset, too, because he is fond of me in his own brotherly way.

It would spoil the companionship we can share.'

She held out her hand to Phil and he took it carefully in his own.

'I'm so sorry, Phil!' she said again.

He gave her his lop-sided smile and said: 'We all have the right to hope. I shall hope that if things don't work out right for you and Dick, you'll turn to me. I wouldn't expect you to love me, Tamily. It would be enough that you'd let me take care of you. Promise me that if the day comes when you really know it is no use, you'll tell me.'

'Phil, that isn't fair to you! It may be years—*years* before Dick marries. I've promised him we'll run the farm together. You can't just sit back and waste all that time...'

'Would you be happy in partnership with Dick—in the circumstances?' Phil asked, wondering.

'Happy?' Tamily gave a wry smile. 'In a way, yes! I'm never more happy—or more sad—than when I'm with Dick. It's wonderful and terrible—both together. It's no good, Phil. I'm not a whole person any more. I couldn't offer you all of me—not ever. I shall always love Dick!'

'I know that!' Phil agreed, surprising her. 'But I could stand it. As for waiting—well, we're all very young still. Five, six, seven years...we'll still only be in our twenties, Tamily. There'd be a whole life-time ahead of us. You can't sit back and resign yourself to spinsterhood at eighteen!'

She smiled, despite her thoughts, just as he had meant her to do.

'Don't you think marriage without love is wrong?' she asked him doubtfully.

'Yes, if it is without love. But I shall love, Tamily. I shall love you always. And I think in a way—not the way you love Dick, of course—you love me a little too. Think how many marriages have less than that and yet are happy. There are so few couples who have more.'

Something told her he was speaking the truth. Mercia and Keith were lucky—they each gave the other all their hearts. How happy Mercia was! She had returned from her honeymoon glowing and radiant. Keith, too, looked the picture of a happy bridegroom. And it would last—Tamily felt sure of that. They were so right for one another. If she *were* to marry Phil, would she have the same look in her eyes, the same radiance as Mercia? Would she be able to share the physical side of marriage with a man she did not love with her whole heart?

She shivered involuntarily.

'I don't know, Phil!' She whispered the words. 'I don't know if I could be a real wife to you.'

If Phil guessed at her thoughts, he did not embarrass her by putting them into words. He said quietly:

'If we were married, Tamily, I would be content just to know you were my wife.'

'You say that now!' Tamily cried. 'But it might not work out that way, Phil. Once I thought it would be enough for me just to be near Dick—sharing his everyday life. But it isn't. It's almost easier when he's nowhere around. Then I can't long for something more. These last few days—when we're alone, I've been happy. It's not the same mad, excited kind of happiness that there is when I'm with Dick, but a peaceful happiness. Sometimes I think I ought to go right away from Allerton Manor, and start a new life.'

'Then why not, Tamily? Marry me and I'll take you away. You can forget Dick—begin again. I'd be there to look after you, help you forget.'

His voice was young, eager, promising so much. For a moment, she was tempted to give way to his dream. A new life—a new start with dear, kind Phil to soften the aloneness, the fear of leaving all that was known and familiar. But almost in the same instant, she knew she could not go. Only two days before she had left for Oxford, Mercia had confided in her in an excited voice:

'Tamily, I think I'm going to have a baby. You're not to tell Keith—nobody knows but you. Keith would worry—you see, he doesn't think I'm strong enough to have children. But I want a baby, Tamily. I want to be able to give Keith a son—it's what he most wants in the world, although he tries to pretend he doesn't mind if we never have any children. If it's true, Tamily, I shall need you near me. I know I couldn't manage a baby on my own. Mother can find herself a proper secretary and you could come and live with us. You'd like that, wouldn't you?'

Tamily had been thrilled and afraid, too. No one had thought of the possibility of Mercia having a child. Obviously such an undertaking might be dangerous for her; Keith himself had said as much. But if

Mercia really wanted a child—and she and Tamily had always loved babies—how wonderful it would be. There would be so much she could do to help Mercia.

She had never thought then that this might happen...this meeting with Phil. A week ago, she would never have believed she might consider for one moment the prospect of going away to a new life as wife to some man other than Dick. She would have called Mercia a lunatic even to imagine such an unlikely event. Yet she had been tempted.

'I'd be running away!' she thought. 'Using Phil as a means of escape! It wouldn't be fair. He was far too nice.'

'I couldn't Phil,' she said gently. 'Not because I don't like you enough—but because I like you far too much to let you make a mess of your life. I know you don't see a future with me as anything but happy—but it would be if you really do love me. We're in the same boat, really. You ought to run away from me—fast, before it becomes a habit. It's just too late, Phil. I'll never stop wanting Dick.'

He tried to hide his disappointment and yet deep down in his heart he knew she was right. When one loved fully, one couldn't discard that love like an outworn coat. It was there, deep down inside, for always. He knew he would never feel this way again about any other girl. He'd never meant to fall in love, but now that it had happened he wasn't sorry. He was only twenty, and he wouldn't have considered marriage yet in any case. He could wait—wait and see what happened to Tamily in the years to come. No matter what she said, she couldn't stop him waiting. Maybe one day she would need him, and then he'd be there.

'I think we should make our way back now,' he said quietly. 'Dick said he would probably drop into my rooms for tea. If he does, I'll make some excuse and leave you alone. I expect you'd like to say good-bye.'

But she wouldn't spoil his last day.

'No,' she said firmly. 'I don't want to see him, Phil. There's no point and, anyway, I'd rather be with you.'

He wasn't sure if she meant it but he was human enough to be pleased and to take her at her word.

'Right, then we'll move on a mile or two downstream. I know a nice riverside café where we can have tea.'

They had barely started the punt once more before a voice hailed them from a passing skiff.

'Hi, love-birds!'

It was Dick and another undergraduate with two young girls. With a sinking heart, Tamily recognized the fair-haired girl from the hotel. So Dick had found her, after all.

THIRTEEN

It was now certain that Mercia was going to have a child. The baby would arrive early in the New Year. It was not as yet noticeable and only Keith and Tamily knew the secret. None of them had yet plucked up the courage to tell Lady Allerton the news.

The two girls were lying in deck chairs in Mercia's garden, the great beech tree shading them from the hot mid-summer sun. Mercia looked pale and drawn but her face still had that glow of radiant happiness which now combined with the peaceful contentment of a woman who carries the child of the man she loves.

'You really must tell your mother soon, Mercia,' Tamily was saying. 'As Keith said at lunch, it won't be long now before she'll be able to see for herself.'

'But she'll fuss so, Tamily, and I'm so happy I can't bear anything to mar it. Even Keith seems to have recovered from the shock and be happy, too.'

Tamily knew this was not so. Last evening when Mercia had retired to bed early as he had ordered her, Keith had confided in Tamily his own deep concern.

'Naturally I haven't told Mercia the truth,' he said with a worried frown, 'but the results of the X-rays aren't too promising. Woods seems to think that she might miscarry and that if she does carry the baby the full term, there might be complications when it's born. She ought not to be having this child.'

Tamily looked at him anxiously.

'But she's so blissfully happy about it, Keith. Are you sure...?'

'Woods is the best gynaecologist in this country,' Keith broke in sharply. 'That's why I took her to him. If anyone can pull her through safely, he will. It's just that I ought never to have allowed her to have this child.'

'I think you're blaming yourself for something which was inevitable,' Tamily said quietly. 'From what Mercia has told me, she knew you were trying to prevent such a thing happening but she wanted to give you a son. In her quiet way, Mercia can be very strong-willed when something matters deeply to her. Even if this baby had not started so soon, I'm quite convinced it was only a matter of time.'

Keith had believed her and indeed, Tamily was sure what she said was true. Now it was up to all of them to see that Mercia rested as much as was possible and that she took no risk at all that might bring on a miscarriage. With Keith's permission, Tamily had warned Mercia about certain eventualities if she did not take care, convinced that this was one way to be sure that Mercia took every opportunity to rest. Fear of losing her baby was about the only thing that would have made her relinquish the task of cooking Keith's meals, answering the telephone for him and generally seeing to his every comfort.

'Where would we all be without you, darling!' Mercia said, sleepily. 'All my life you seem to have been hovering somewhere near me, spoiling me.'

'I love to do it,' Tamily said quickly, 'and when the baby comes, you'll be lucky to get even a look at him. I shall be a domineering and possessive nanny who only allows the fond mamma a brief look at her offspring once a day!'

Mercia laughed.

'I shall be only too glad to let you minister to the little angel,' she said happily. 'I wouldn't know one end of a baby from the other. After all those books you've been studying, you ought to be an expert.'

It was Tamily's turn to smile.

'I'm sure babies, like everything else, are quite different when it comes to practice, not theory,' she said. 'Since you're insisting on me as a nanny, Mercia, it's as well you married a doctor. We'll have to get Keith to draw up a baby time-table or we shall spoil him hopelessly between us.'

Quite unconsciously she had adopted Mercia's pronoun for the child. Mercia never seemed to doubt her child was going to be a boy—the son that Keith wanted.

'Did you tell Dick?' Mercia asked suddenly. 'I wonder how he'll like being an uncle?'

'I haven't written recently,' Tamily replied awkwardly. 'But I will get a letter off tomorrow.'

'Too busy writing to the new boy-friend!' Mercia teased her.

Tamily blushed. It was true that she had been keeping up a regular correspondence with Phil, but they were not love-letters. Phil wrote mainly of his work and leisure-time activities. He always included a paragraph about Dick as if he understood only too well that she was desperate for news of him. His last letter had indicated how thoughtful he was of her feelings, for until then there had been no mention of Dick's friendship with the fair-haired girl.

...I believe Dick's blonde has finally given up trying to dazzle Dick with her charms. He told me yesterday that she had departed home to mamma and that he was quite glad to be rid of her as she had become embarrassingly affectionate. He said if I was writing, to send you his love.

Tamily felt as if for years now she had watched Dick falling in and out of love and bitterly she wondered who the next one would be. She didn't have to wait long. The afternoon brought with it a long letter in Dick's untidy scrawl telling her in detail of the incredible new girl of his life.

Of course, I wouldn't dream of letting Mother know what's going on! he wrote. *Dorice is hardly up to Mother's social standards but I find her wonderfully refreshing after all those Commem debs. At least Dorice says what she means, and means what she says. She's only seventeen but she's been around a good deal and the poor kid had to leave school when she was fifteen and has been working as a hairdresser ever since. I can see what she means when she says her 'vital statistics' have been a handicap rather than an asset! I gather young and old fall over themselves like ninepins to get somewhere with her and she's pretty cynical about men generally. I feel sorry for her because she's led a pretty unromantic life up to now, losing her job because the boss won't take 'no' for an answer, and getting chucked out from home because some fellow deliberately ran out of petrol and kept her out all night. One has to admire a girl like Dorice for coming through the sordid side of life and yet remaining so innocent. Thank God I'm not a snob, and can appreciate Dorice for what she really is.*

How are things progressing between you and Phil? Whenever I drop into his rooms he always seems to be in the throes of an emotional outpouring on paper, which I gather is addressed to you. He's really a very decent chap, Tammy, and I do hope something comes out of it, although not too soon. Don't forget I want help starting up Lower Beeches and I certainly shan't give any consent to your marrying for quite a few years yet.

I'm thinking of inviting Phil home for part of the summer vac. What say you?

As ever, your loving Dick.

Well, Mercia's condition would give her sufficient excuse to prevent Phil's coming. She would have no time for keeping Phil or Dick company this coming vacation between her duties at Allerton Manor and running Mercia's home for her. Moments like these when she could sit down and relax were few and far between.

She thought Mercia was asleep, but she seemed to open her eyes suddenly and said:

'I think I shall call him Dick. Funnily enough, it was Keith's father's name—Richard, anyway. But Richard seems a bit of a mouthful for a little baby. Tamily...'

She turned suddenly to face her friend.

'What's happening between you and Dick? You seem somehow different since Oxford. You didn't fall for Dick's friend by any chance?'

Tamily shook her head.

'I liked him a lot, Mercia. If it hadn't been for Dick...' she broke off, unhappily.

Mercia sighed.

'I wish I could knock some sense into that brother of mine. Wasn't he the least bit jealous that you spent so much time with Phil?'

'Dick was far too busy with his own affairs,' Tamily replied quietly. 'And you're not to worry about me, Mercia. These last few months have passed very happily and I really haven't the slightest desire to get married.'

Mercia stared up at the cloudless blue sky, thoughtfully.

'Perhaps all women as happily married as I want to see their girl-friends married, too,' she said. 'Sometimes I feel frightened, Tamily. It all seems too good to be true. When you open your daily newspaper you read such terrible things—death and disaster, tragedy and unhappiness. I feel

199

as if I had no right to have so much happiness. You don't think I'm going to lose my baby, do you?'

'No, no of course not,' Tamily said quickly. 'Keith told me only yesterday that by the end of this month the worst danger of miscarrying will be over. Provided you do as you're told and obey Keith implicity. I'm sure everything will be all right.'

Mercia relaxed once more.

'Yes, that's what *I* feel. Somehow, deep down inside me, I *know* I'm going to have this baby. I know that it's going to be a boy and I know he'll be perfect. But don't ask me how I know—Keith would say woman's intuition, I suppose.'

Tamily held her breath. It was almost as if Mercia were daring the fates to come between her and what her heart desired. It mustn't happen. It mustn't! Pray God that Mercia was right and that the baby would wait its time and all would be well.

'I'll tell Mother tomorrow,' Mercia said dreamily. 'I expect Father will be pleased with the idea of a grandson. If it is a boy, I expect Father will help Keith and me with his education. He's sure to want him to go to his old school and follow Dick up to Oxford. I must ask Keith if he'd mind.'

'Mind what, darling?'

Keith startled them both by his unexpected appearance. He flung himself down on the grass at Mercia's feet and looked up at her with unashamed adoration.

Mercia told him.

'Of course I wouldn't mind, darling,' was his forceful reply. Tamily felt that he might well have added... 'I don't care about anything except that you should be all right.'

Then she rose to her feet and said: 'I'll go and get you both some tea and we'll have it out here on the lawn.'

But when she returned they were sitting quietly in the sunshine, holding hands, and unwilling to intrude excused herself saying she must go back to the Manor to see to the flowers for the dinner-table.

There was in fact little for her to do at Allerton Manor. Lady Allerton was out playing Bridge and the dinner guests would not be arriving until eight o'clock.

Tamily went to her room and tried to concentrate on her new library book. She had not read through the first chapter when she heard the telephone in the hall. Always, nowadays, her mind shot to Mercia but she quelled the fear quickly, knowing that nothing could have happened in the short hour since she had left Mercia resting in the sunshine in Keith's care. She lifted the receiver with disinterest and was surprised to hear Dick's voice.

'Thank heavens it's you, Tammy. I've been trying to get through for nearly an hour.'

'What's the matter, Dick? Something must be wrong for you to phone home at such an hour?'

'I'm in a hell of a mess. Are you alone? Can I talk to you? Mother's not around, is she?'

Tamily quickly reassured him.

'It's Dorice,' Dick said in answer to her repeated question. 'I don't know what to do with her, Tammy. She tried to kill herself last night and I haven't dared leave her. I'm phoning from her digs now.'

White-faced, Tamily stared at the mouthpiece.

'But why? *Why?*' she asked. 'You'd better tell me everything, Dick.'

His voice came surprisingly close and distinct. He might almost have been in the same room.

'She's going to have a baby. She wants me to marry her, but I can't. I know I

202

ought to, Tammy, but I just can't go through with it. I'm not in love with her and I don't honestly think she's in love with me. She's just scared out of her wits. There isn't a soul here in Oxford she can turn to. Her people won't have her back and she hasn't anyone but me. I've got to be back in Hall tonight and I daren't leave her alone.'

He sounded desperate. For the moment only this seemed real to her. Everything else he said was so incredible, so impossible, that she couldn't believe it.

'Are you still there, Tammy?'

'Yes, yes I'm here,' she replied. 'Tell me what you want me to do, Dick.'

'I thought if you could come up and be with her. Somehow or other, I can get it sorted out, but I can't leave her alone now. She says she'll have another try to end her life if I do. For God's sake, Tammy, come and help me if you possibly can.'

She knew she would go. How she would deal with the situation she had no idea. That didn't matter. What mattered was that Dick had asked for her help and somehow she must find a way to give it.

'I'll come on the next train,' she said

quietly, and cutting short his thanks quickly replaced the receiver. She knew she would have to tell someone that she was going away for the night. At any other time, she would have gone to Mercia. She turned now to her mother, showing her first Dick's letter and then telling her about the telephone call. Jess listened quietly until Tamily had finished. Then she said:

'You're quite sure you want to get involved?'

'Dick says...'

'So you're definitely going?' Jess broke in. What Dick said would always govern what Tamily did. Jess knew it and accepted the inevitable. 'Then listen to me, Tamily. Without speaking to the girl I can't be absolutely sure, but it sounds to me as if this Dorice is playing rather a dangerous game with young Dick. I think she wants to force him into marriage. He'd be quite a catch for a girl like her, and she probably knows she hasn't a hope any other way. I doubt she's going to have a baby. Yes, I doubt it very much.'

'But Dick said...'

Once again, Jess broke in on her daughter.

'I've no doubt the young fool has been hoodwinked,' she said sharply. 'It's you I'm warning, Tamily. If you want to get Dick out of this mess you've got to play the game her way—call her bluff. Pretend you believe there is a baby; pretend that as a relative of Dick's—his sister if you like—you feel it's his duty to make an honest woman of her. At the same time, you think he's young to be getting married and that for both their sakes the best thing they can do is to find out for sure that there really is a baby on the way. Naturally, you won't doubt her word, but people can make mistakes about such things and no doubt this Dorice would welcome positive proof one way or another just as much as Dick. You will, therefore, accompany her to the Radcliffe Infirmary in Oxford for a test.'

She saw the lack of comprehension in her young daughter's eyes.

'You don't know what that is! It's perfectly simple. Dorice will have to supply a specimen. If the reaction is positive, it will be certain she's having a child. A negative reaction is not always certain but I hardly think you need concern yourself with this. It is my own belief that long before you get to the hospital, Dorice will call it all off.'

'And if it's genuine?' Tamily asked. 'If it's all true, what shall we do then?'

Jess smiled grimly. 'We'll worry about that if and when the time comes,' she replied. 'Now pack your suitcase and be off, Tamily. And don't forget what I've told you. You and Dick are a couple of soft-hearted, credulous young fools and this time you'll just have to harden your hearts.'

'You'll tell Lady Allerton where I've gone?' Tamily asked.

'Indeed, I shall do no such thing,' was Jess's calm reply. 'I shall probably tell her that one of your relatives is ill.'

Tamily gave her mother an impulsive hug. It was not often she went to Jess for help, but whenever she did it was wonderfully forthcoming.

The two-hour journey to Oxford seemed unending. When at last she arrived, hot and dusty from the airless railway carriage, there was no one to meet her. She realized with a sinking heart that she had forgotten to take down the address of Dorice's rooms. Obviously Dick had no intention of leaving her alone, so it was useless to telephone the College...unless she could get hold of Phil. Dick might possibly have thought of this eventuality, and rung his friend.

With some difficulty she managed to get through to Phil. Immediately he gave her the address and asked her if she would like him to go with her.

'Dick didn't tell me what it was all about, but if I can help I will.'

She would have liked to have him beside her, but it was not for her to betray Dick's confidence and reluctantly she declined his offer, promising to get in touch with him as soon as she was free to do so.

Two minutes later, she was in a taxi, passing familiar streets, the hotel where she had stayed, Dick's college, and at last to the far side of the town. The taxi driver pulled up outside a rather dingy boarding-house. She paid him off and rang the doorbell.

The front door stood ajar and Tamily walked in. She stood around for a moment uncertainly, looking for the number of Dorice's room, and then an upstairs door banged and a dishevelled, untidy Dick clattered down the stairs to greet her.

'Thank God you've come, Tam,' he said, violently. 'I don't know what to do with her.'

'I'll deal with it,' Tamily said quietly. 'You can go back to College, Dick. I'll telephone you as soon as I can.'

Dick started to argue but she put a restraining hand on his arm.

'I'd rather cope alone,' she said quietly.

He tried not to look too relieved but clearly he could not wait to be out of the house and away from the sordid atmosphere into which he seemed to have got himself. She felt curiously numb. She knew she ought to feel shocked, horrified, at what had happened. But even though she was here in the house, it didn't seem real. It was as if she were reading some magazine story and presently would turn a page and find out what happened next. But the scene which met her eyes as she opened Dorice's door was real enough. It was a shambles. Magazines, gramophone records, empty chocolate boxes, lay scatterd about the plush hair sofa and chairs. Unwashed glasses and a half-consumed bottle of gin were on the coffee table, together with a layer of dust. It looked as if nothing had been cleaned or swept or polished in months.

Disgust welled up in her and with an effort she looked beyond the sitting-room to the bedroom door.

'Dick, is that you?'

The girl's strident, nasal tones spoke sharply through the open doorway.

Tamily grasped her white handbag more tightly and stepped forward.

Her first feeling was one of pure surprise. Dick had said Dorice was seventeen. The girl in the crimson georgette nightdress must have been approaching thirty, even allowing for the streaked make-up and red-rimmed eyes that stared back at her with equal surprise.

'Who the hell are you?'

Concealing her revulsion, Tamily stepped forward and held out her hand.

'I'm Dick's sister,' she said quickly. 'I've come to help you, Dorice.'

The girl did not take the proffered hand but stared at Tamily suspiciously.

'Did Dick ask you to come?'

Tamily nodded.

'He's very concerned about you, Dorice. He thought you ought to have someone with you at a time like this.'

The girl looked at her expectantly.

'So you know—about the baby, I mean?'

'I know you and Dick are both worried in case you should be pregnant,' Tamily corrected her.

Deep down inside, Tamily knew that this girl had not really tried to take her life. She was remarkably self-possessed; there was no sign of hysteria in her voice and although she now put a handkerchief up to her eyes, Tamily could see no sign of tears.

'He must marry me. He must!' Dorice was crying in a loud, theatrical voice. 'If he doesn't, I'll kill myself, I swear I will.'

Tamily knew then that her mother was right. A trap had been set, but Dick was not caught yet and he wasn't going to be.

Remembering Jess's advice, she told Dorice exactly why she had come.

Tears forgotten, Dorice swung round to face Tamily, her eyes hard and fearful.

'But that's not necessary. I *know* I'm pregnant. I don't need any blasted test to prove it to me. You can't prove I'm not.'

'Nor can you prove at this stage that

you are!' Tamily replied. She was almost enjoying herself now. This woman would have ruined Dick's life without a qualm. She felt no pity for her, not even dislike.

'And if I have this test, and the result says I'm pregnant, you'll make him marry me?'

Tamily was momentarily afraid. If Dorice was willing to go through with it, perhaps she was right after all. She nodded her head, unwilling to speak the lie.

Dorice gave a slow, satisfied smile.

'All right. Then I'll have the test tomorrow. Shall I let you or Dick know the result?'

Tamily felt as if her whole being was flooded with relief. It wasn't true. Dorice had been going to lie once more.

'Dick will be busy in College, tomorrow. He's taking exams, you know. But you're not to worry about a thing, Dorice. I shall come with you to the hospital, so you won't be alone.'

Beneath the sun-tan make-up, still patchy on her cheeks, Dorice paled.

'But I don't need no one to go with me,' she faltered.

'I wouldn't dream of letting you go alone,' Tamily replied smoothly. 'I've made an appointment for ten o'clock tomorrow morning, in my name. I didn't think you would want your name involved.'

It wasn't the first time she'd lied for Dick. There'd been so many now that it rolled smoothly off her tongue, convincing even Dorice of its validity.

Dorice clapped her hands to her mouth.

'But I can't...I won't...' Quite suddenly her face crumpled, and for the first time the tears were genuine.

Tamily waited a moment, listening to the girl's choked sobs.

'It's no good, Dorice,' she said, gently but firmly. 'Dick may look as if he were born yesterday, but he's not quite the fool you might suppose. He never believed that there was going to be a baby, but he wasn't sure just how desperate you were. I shouldn't try to fake another suicide. He won't be taken in again.'

Dorice swung round and faced Tamily with a cruel, spiteful look.

'Get out!' She spat the words viciously in Tamily's direction. 'Get out, damn you! Get out, get out!'

She was still screaming after her as Tamily hurried quickly from the room, down the stairs and out into the glorious

212

fresh air. She stood for a moment feeling the cool evening breeze against her hot cheeks and breathed deeply before she turned and began to walk towards the centre of the town.

She knew she ought to telephone Dick, put him out of his misery, but bitterly she decided that it wouldn't do him any harm to let him suffer a little longer.

Was he never going to grow up? Was she to spend her grown-up life as she had as a child, getting him out of scrapes so that he never really bore the brunt of his misdeeds? Something deep within her left her sickened at the thought of Dick and that girl. How could he?

She tried to see Dorice through Dick's eyes. *'Wonderfully refreshing after all the debs!'* No doubt Dorice *was* a contrast. *'She says what she means and means what she says...she's only seventeen...poor kid had to leave school when she was fifteen...vital statistics...'* Well, she hadn't had time to notice those, but no doubt a Dorice got up for the man-hunt could be devastating to a susceptible young man.

Phil wouldn't...but then, Phil was in love with her. Dick didn't know the meaning of the word *love*. He was still chasing after the novel, the sensational, the glamour. He would grow up. He must grow up one of these days. She turned to a nearby telephone kiosk and dialled Phil's number.

FOURTEEN

Phil was wonderful. The relief of letting him take charge of her was enormous. She hadn't realized under what a strain she had been all afternoon. Now reaction had set in and had it not been for Phil's capable presence she felt she might indeed have gone to pieces.

He had booked her a room in the Mitre, even managing to obtain the same room so that she would be in familiar surroundings. Somehow he had managed to do this before coming on his bicycle to collect her from the telephone kiosk where he had told her to wait for him. He had asked no questions except to inquire if she wished him to bring Dick back to the hotel for dinner.

Tamily felt she couldn't bear to see Dick; and Phil, bless him, seemed to understand.

They sat in the lounge drinking large cups of black coffee and tired though she was, Tamily felt the warmth and life coming back to her mind and body.

'That's better!' Phil said, seeing her smile at some remark he had made.

Suddenly she felt able to talk about the day's events. She wanted to be able to relieve herself of the horror and revulsion and the nervous tension that still remained as an aftermath. But in the same moment she knew it was not her secret to reveal. If Dick had wanted Phil to know, he could have confided in him long since. Perhaps Dick was too ashamed to let anyone as decent as Phil know how he had been behaving.

As if sensing the trend of her thoughts, Phil said:

'However awful the circumstances which brought you here, Tamily, I can't help feeling grateful for them. It's been wonderful seeing you so unexpectedly. I must confess I'd been hoping I might be able to persuade you to lunch and a show in Town during the summer vac. Would you come, Tamily?'

She hesitated for the fraction of a second. It would be so nice to have a day in Town with Phil, but there was Mercia to think about first. Briefly she told Phil the facts. As always, he seemed to understand how she felt although he protested mildly.

'I wonder if the day will ever come, Tamily, when you'll put yourself before others?' he remarked, thoughtfully.

Tamily smiled.

'One day, Phil, you're going to take off those rose-coloured spectacles and get quite a shock. I'm not so unselfish as you might suppose. It's just that I would never forgive myself if I weren't there when Mercia needed me. Even if I did not love her so much, I couldn't forget how much I owe to her—to all the Allertons. I've had a wonderful childhood and been brought up in circumstances that would never have been possible if my mother hadn't been given this chance for us both.'

It became suddenly vitally necessary to tell Phil about her mother's past. She needed to know just how much her own illegitimacy mattered. Mercia had said that it made no difference but naturally dear, kind Mercia would say anything to help to make her happy.

She watched Phil's face carefully for his reactions. There was no horror, no withdrawal, only the wonderful under- standing and sympathy she was beginning to expect from him.

'You make yourself sound like a reformed criminal confessing to past crimes,' he chided her gently. 'As if any of it were your fault, Tamily! I know this probably isn't the time and place to burden you with my feelings, but what you've told me only makes me all the more sure I want to marry you.'

He hurried on before she could interrupt him, saying:

'I know nothing has changed. The way you turned up today only proves you're as much in love with Dick as ever. What I've said just now wasn't a proposal to which you must give me a "yes" or "no"; it was just a statement of fact.'

She had never come nearer to loving him than she did at that moment. Gratitude, as well as pity, was pulling at her heart, and she wished above all that for both their sakes she could bring herself to say that she would marry him. With unusual perceptiveness, Tamily could foresee her future as Phil's wife. There would be a steady, dependable affection, a quiet companionship, a care for one another's feelings and complete security for her. Phil would be incapable of letting anyone down, least of all his wife. Life would proceed through clearly foreseeable channels; a small home somewhere in the country, Phil as History Master at some boys' school, perhaps; children; holidays together at the seaside and the quiet, steady years of their old age. No doubt there were many women who demanded no more for a perfect marriage. Perhaps if there had been no Dick she might have accepted that pattern for herself, but could she ever accept it now? She would always be conscious of the one great missing factor—love. Married to Dick, there might be no security, no guarantee as to the future, not even the comforting certainly of his love for her enduring through the years. But the loss seemed as nothing when she envisaged the homecoming of her heart to its rightful place. There might be heartaches, tears, disappointments and little peace. But everything would be bearable to know she had the right to love and care for him for the rest of their lives.

'I'm sorry, Phil. I wish I could say "yes". I wish I could marry you, but I can't believe it is right either for you or for me. You need a whole woman, some girl who can offer you all her heart and not just a broken, useless one.'

Even as she spoke she knew that, given the chance, Phil would want to try to mend her heart, be willing to put up with second best. Phil loved her in the same way as she loved Dick, giving all and asking nothing in return; each grateful for the crumbs that came their way.

Phil leaned over to pour her another cup of coffee. He gave her his one-sided smile and said with forced cheerfulness: 'Tell me more about Dick's sister,' realizing that this was a topic dear to Tamily's heart.

'She sounds a sweet person,' he said when she had fully described Mercia. 'As different from my own sister as chalk from cheese.'

Something in Phil's voice told her that he and Anthea did not share the same deep affection as did Dick and Mercia.

'Anthea is frightfully brainy,' Phil was saying. 'She got a First in Classics last year with no trouble at all. I have to swot like hell to pass any exam. I suppose some people would say she's too clever for a woman. It gives a man an inferiority complex to be with her—at least, it does

219

me. She gets along all right with Father, of course, because he's even brainier than she is. Did I tell you they're going off to Libya? They've managed to get a permit from the Government to explore in the ruins of Cyrene. They'll be in their element there. As far as I can gather from their conversation, the first settlers arrived there the beginning of the seventh century B.C. That ought to be far enough back for them. They wanted me to go with them, at least Father did, but I'd rather stay on and take my degree. History fascinates me, but only modern history. I don't seem able to generate any interest for ancient ruins and mummified Pharaohs.'

She laughed, at ease once more in his company.

'Is Anthea pretty?' she asked, interested in Phil's sister after his description of her profundity.

'I suppose it's rather hard for a brother to judge. I don't think she could be described as pretty. As a kid, she was rather plain but she's very tall now, rather distinguished-looking; dark, with long, slanting eyes. I think she deliberately cultivates an Egyptian look. I know she firmly believes she's reincarnated from a princess of ancient Egypt. Of course, I think that's only a lot of rot. But one has to admit that she does look the part. It's partly her eyes and partly the way she does her hair—her clothes, too.'

'She sounds very unusual,' Tamily said, smiling.

Phil shrugged his shoulders.

'I suppose she is. But there's something odd about Anthea. Men seem to fall madly in love with her and then cool off. I'm never quite sure if she does it deliberately or if they get scared by her. I can't see her as a wife and mother. Of course, she's only twenty-two and this burning obsession for archaeology may well give way to more normal, feminine aspirations as time goes by.'

A waiter came across the room and stopped beside Tamily.

'You are wanted on the telephone, Miss.'

Tamily's heart missed a beat. *'Mercia!'* she thought, and then realized that the call couldn't have come from home. No one knew she was staying at this hotel. It could only be Dick.

Phil must have reached the same conclusion, for he said, anxiously:

221

'Would you like me to take the call for you, Tamily?'

She shook her head.

'I've got to put his mind at rest. He won't be able to work properly while he's worrying.'

Dick's voice was distorted over the wire and, strangely, he sounded farther away then he had done when he called her at home.

'Tammy! I rang you as soon as I could get out of Hall. I'd have skipped it altogether and blown the consequences except Phil said you were a bit tired and wanted a rest. He said you didn't feel like talking about anything. But I must know! He gave me your message. Just to say there was no need to worry.'

The calmness of her own voice surprised her. Already the nightmare vision of Dorice in that sordid room was receding into the past.

'You won't see Dorice again, Dick. There never was a child. She just coveted your title.'

'No baby?' Dick repeated stupidly. 'But she said... That's why she tried to kill herself...' He broke off uncertainly.

'She never had the slightest intention of

222

taking her life,' Tamily reassured him. 'She fooled you nicely, Dick. I don't suppose you would have been the first to be caught in the same trap. You'd better be more careful next time.'

She couldn't withhold the last bitter remark. There was a slight pause, and then Dick said:

'There won't be a next time, Tammy. I've finished with women. It seems I can only pick the rotten ones. You've been a brick, Tammy. I can't tell you how grateful I am.'

'I didn't do it for you!' Tamily lied. 'It was to save your family the disgrace. I don't doubt you would have been sent down if there'd been anything in Dorice's story.'

'Don't lecture me, Tammy. I know I deserve it but I've had just about as much as I can stand. You don't know what the last forty-eight hours have been like.'

'But I can guess,' Tamily thought wryly, remembering Dick's appearance when he had rushed out to meet her on the landing that evening. She relented. No doubt he'd paid the price of his folly.

'Let's forget it!' she said, more gently.

'I've got some news for you, Dick—about Mercia.'

She told him about Mercia's baby and he sounded genuinely thrilled at the idea of becoming an uncle, but close on his delight came his concern, never far absent from his thoughts, for Mercia.

'She's going to be all right? Keith's not worried about her?'

Tamily decided not to tell him the whole truth. He had another week of exams before the vac, and there would be time enough then to tell him how worried they all were.

'She's under the best gynaecologist there is,' she told him quietly. 'There's no cause to worry.'

Dick's voice sounded suddenly very young again, fired with the old boyish enthusiasm.

'Gosh, Tam, just think of it! Mercia with a baby. Seems fantastic!'

'How quickly he gets over anything unpleasant,' Tamily thought, not without a shade of bitterness. 'Now that he has no cause to be afraid, he can put Dorice and all that unpleasantness behind him.' If only she, too, could forget it had ever happened. Would she ever be able to look Dick straight in the face again? It was the first really unpleasant thing she had known Dick to be concerned with. His escapades as a boy had been no more than a wholesome mischievousness that in itself was lovable. His association with Sylvie had hurt her but Dick was the injured party and had lost no more than a little dignity. But this—this affair with Dorice...

She tried, angrily, to put away that horrible thought of him lying there beside that woman...she pulled herself up sharply. She had read enough modern literature to know that young men nowadays were not expected to lead celibate lives. It never had been expected of a man. These were the years when they were supposed to sow their wild oats. How wrong that someone like her mother should suffer the consequences of this unfair rule of society—one law for the men and another for the women.

'Tammy, couldn't I come round and see you, talk to you?' Dick's voice interrupted her thoughts.

'No!' she said quickly. And then: 'I'm sorry, Dick, but I'm dreadfully tired. It's late. I'm just going to bed.'

'Then can I see you tomorrow morning?

I can probably get out between lectures for elevenses.'

She hadn't thought about it before, but she knew now she would take the first train home. There was nothing to stay for. She didn't want to see Dick and it was better for Phil if she didn't see him, either.

Dick didn't argue with her. He thanked her again and sent his love to his family, in particular to Mercia. She didn't trouble to tell him that no one knew she was here except Jess.

'See you in a fortnight, then,' Dick said cheerfully. 'And Tammy, I'll never forget what you've done for me today—not as long as I live.'

She tried to find comfort in those words but there was none. It wasn't gratitude she wanted from Dick, it was his love...

FIFTEEN

Tamily knew she had never been so happy in her life before. The hot weather had begun in earnest the first day of the summer vac, and one long, lazy, sunny day had followed upon another. It was almost as if time had no meaning and she and Mercia and Dick were back in their childhood again.

Keith was terribly busy. He would be hard at work from early morning until late at night and the three of them spent the days together just as they had so often done when Dick was home from school.

Mercia was as much confined to her deck-chair as once she had been to her wheel-chair. The gynaecologist had advised total rest for her. To another woman, this might have been a period of boredom and endurance, but for Mercia the familiar restriction held no hardships. She would sit happily, watching Dick and Tamily play a game of tennis or wander off together down to the stream to swim, but they never left her alone for long. Presently they would be back, laughing, chatting, keeping her amused. Even when she was alone, she was never bored. Close beside her chair she had her work-basket and her small, delicate hands would be busy embroidering something dainty and diaphanous for her baby's layette.

Watching her, Tamily realized how true

the saying was that a woman never looked more beautiful than when she was carrying a child. Mercia had never looked more fit, either. Her thin, pale face had filled out and her cheeks were rosy and glowing with good health. It seemed fantastic that Keith or the specialist could still be worrying about her. Tamily, herself, had no further worries. The dangerous first three months had gone, and she was now as convinced as Mercia that the baby would be safely delivered.

Neither she nor Dick would leave until the tired but contented Keith arrived home. Then they would wander back to the Manor for dinner, or perhaps down to Lower Beeches to see the foal, now a strong young colt.

Dick was full of plans and schemes for the future. The past and Dorice were never mentioned. Surprising them all, he had heard that he had passed his intermediate B.A. It was typical of Dick that without much effort he'd passed his exams with flying colours. Tamily had been momentarily reminded of Phil's sister, Anthea, who seemed to have the same gift.

In a fortnight's time, Phil would be

bringing Anthea to stay at the Manor. When Dick had first suggested it, Tamily had been against the idea. She and Mercia and Dick were so happy. She didn't want even so nice a person as Phil intruding, far less the unknown Anthea.

But Mercia had finally persuaded her.

'You know Dick, Tammy. He loves life and people and lots going on around him. Besides, I'm dying to meet this Phil of yours. From the little you've told me about him, I'm beginning to think that you might end up preferring him to that hopeless brother of mine. And if you are still breaking your heart over Dick, what better way to bring him to his senses than by having an admirer on the spot?'

Tamily was not sorry now that Phil was coming. She enjoyed his company and she knew that Mercia would like him. But Anthea...she couldn't think of any one reason why she should be afraid of her coming. The fact that Anthea was brainy was not really to be worried about—she could no doubt enjoy the lazy summer days as much as anyone else, or if she were bored she could read or go and study the ruins of Allerton Castle. They might not be ancient Roman ruins but they were relics of William the Conqueror's day and well worth viewing. And surely there was no need for Tamily to fear her as a rival for Dick's time and attention. Phil had said that Anthea had little interest in men and that men did not seem to care for her for long. Perhaps it was just that life was complete without Phil or Anthea. But she must not be selfish or possessive about the two people who were dearest in the world to her.

Because she felt guilty about her true feelings, Tamily made an extra effort the day before their arrival to ensure their welcome. She took especial trouble arranging the beautiful, exotic orchids that Burroughs seemed to be able to grow in profusion in the greenhouse. She felt sure that these strange Eastern flowers would appeal to Anthea, and placed a vase of them on her bed-table. In Phil's room she had put one or two carefully-chosen books and several ashtrays, since he was seldom without his pipe.

Dick, coming upon her whilst she performed these tasks, teased her unmercifully.

'Must make sure the boy friend's got all he wants. Perhaps you'd like to lend him some of my hair lotion?'

He wandered past her and stared out of the window of the guest room.

'I say, Tammy, I wonder what his sister's really like? I do hope she's not going to be a crashing bore. All this reincarnation and carry-on sounds a bit cranky to me.'

But Anthea, when at last she arrived, was not in the least what any of them had expected. She fitted Phil's physical description of her—tall, pale, very dark, with slanting brown eyes and her hair coiled on top of her head. She had the straight, classic features of the Egyptian woman and Tamily was forced to admit that the girl had been clever to accentuate this unusual facet of her appearance. With a more normal hair-style, her long straight nose might have been ugly, the mouth too wide and thin. Similarly, her tall, rather angular, body might have seemed awkward and unfeminine. As it was, the effect she produced was startling. The straight, white linen tunic dress had been a wonderful choice to complement the Grecian-Egyptian effect. Even the hem of the skirt had been embroidered with the Greek key pattern in a startling amber shade. Rows of bangles jangled on her long, bare, white arms and Tamily noticed a tiny gold chain round one slender ankle. Her bare toes, painted a bright scarlet, showed startlingly through the white leather sandals.

Beside her, Tamily heard Dick draw in his breath in started surprise.

'I say, Phil,' he said, turning to his friend, 'you might have told us she was such a stunner!'

If Anthea was pleased by the compliment, she gave no sign. She stood completely silent and Tamily had the impression that any moment now she might clap those long, tapering, white hands to call her retinue of slaves.

Dick, it seemed, was more than ready to be one of them.

'Let me show you your room,' he said to Anthea, bustling around her, picking up her suitcase and beauty bag. 'I'm sure you'd like a wash and clean-up before tea.'

Anthea inclined her head, but still said nothing. Tamily stood with Phil, watching her follow Dick up the wide staircase. Beside her, Phil said warmly: 'It's awfully good to see you again, Tamily. You're looking wonderfully well.'

She turned and accepted the hand he held out to her. 'It's nice to see you too, Phil,' she replied truthfully. 'I hope this wonderful weather will hold. There's so much I want to be able to show you.'

He walked with her to the french windows and out on to the terrace. It was blazing hot and the heady smell from the rose garden hung about the air, mingling with the wistaria on the mellowed brick walls of the Manor House.

'It's the most beautiful place!' he said, with genuine admiration. 'No wonder you don't want to leave it, Tamily. I can understand now why you were always in such a hurry to get home. Dick never told me much about the place, and your own descriptions were inadequate. It's all so much bigger and more beautiful than I had imagined.'

Simmonds came through the door behind them carrying the massive silver tea-tray and presently Dick and Anthea joined them on the terrace. Anthea immediately seated herself in one of the garden chairs beneath the brightly-coloured sun-umbrella. 'It is obvious she didn't belong to the sect of sun-worshippers,' Tamily thought, not without humour. But no doubt that dead-white skin might burn easily and Anthea was wise to protect herself from it.

As she handed round the plate of cucumber sandwiches, Tamily found herself musing on the thought of Anthea amongst the ruins in the Libyan desert. How was she going to manage to keep out of the sun there? Or would she wear one of those incredible solar topees? The kind one associated with tourists in hot countries.

Tamily felt a nervous desire to giggle. There was something forbidding about Anthea, something strange, dedicated, unfathomable.

Dick, however, didn't seem in the least awed. He was engaging her in conversation with his customary easy charm, bringing an occasional smile to that wide mouth, even a look of animation to the immobile face. After tea, they strolled down to the Dower House so that Phil and Anthea could meet Mercia. Tamily was relieved when in a moment alone with her Mercia said:

'I like your Phil, darling, but his sister scares me to death.'

'So it's not just me, jealous again because Dick likes her,' Tamily thought.

Her natural wish to be fair made her seek out Anthea's company and try to get to know Phil's sister better. But conversation between the two girls never flowed easily. Anthea would listen to Tamily's comments and reply politely enough, but did not further the topic and left the younger girl with the feeling that such small talk was unnecessary, and beneath her. She was not really a difficult guest, neither demanding nor unwilling to fit in with the general plans, but her acquiescence seemed to Tamily to savour always of condescension. She was not exactly bored, and yet one had the feeling that boredom was never far away. Dick, alone, seemed to have the power to draw her out. With him, she would converse freely, and the topic was always archaeology. Amazed, Tamily heard Dick discuss the subject with an enthusiastic interest. After a few days, he was even making serious comments which Tamily could not know he had gleaned from a book on Ancient Egypt which Anthea had lent to him.

Slowly and painfully she was forced to realize that Dick was 'smitten'. It wasn't the same boyish adoration he'd had for Sylvie, nor the elemental desire for Dorice. This time he was on equal terms with a woman—the few years difference in their ages was scarcely noticeable.

Even Phil seemed surprised.

'I'd never have thought those two would hit it off!' he told her, as they walked down the drive to tea with Mercia. Dick and Anthea had gone to see Allerton Castle together. 'They're such complete opposites, and Dick—well, he sometimes seems such a boy still. Anthea has never been young, not even when she was a little girl. What surprises me most of all is her interest in Dick. The usual practice is to collect a scalp, add it to her collection and then drop the victim like a hot brick.'

He seemed to remember, suddenly, that he was talking to the girl who was in love with Dick, and he said quickly:

'I'm damned sorry, Tamily. I'd never have brought her if I'd have known this was going to happen. You looked so happy and pleased with life when we arrived. Now you look miserable.'

'Please, Phil, don't!' she begged him. 'I don't care, really I don't. I've known all along that Dick doesn't love me and I'm used to this kind of thing now. If he's got to marry anyone, I'd just as soon it was your sister.'

Phil smiled down at her.

'I shall take that as the compliment I hope you intended,' he said, 'but I doubt very much if it's going to be that serious. I don't believe Anthea will ever get married. She'll certainly never give up the idea of this expedition with Father—they've been planning it for years. Dick would have to chuck Oxford and go with her, unless of course they decided to wait and get married when she comes back. But already she and Father are talking about an expedition to New Guinea the year after. Can you honestly see Dick trailing round ruins and mulling over bits of bone? I can't!'

'He seems to be happy mulling round ruins this afternoon!' Tamily said wryly. 'I suppose it's a kind of bug that can get you, like stamp-collecting or heraldry. Dick doesn't seem to care whether he gets his degree or not.'

She picked a twig from the roadside and swished it aimlessly through the hot air.

'Oh, don't let's talk about it, Phil. Let's not think about tomorrow. It's such a beautiful day today.'

But this once he couldn't give way, even to please her.

'If what you said just now is true, Tamily,

and you have really resigned yourself to the fact that Dick might never love you, surely there is some hope for me, after all?'

Tamily scuffed her sandalled feet in the dry, dusty rubble of the road. Absurdly, the gesture pleased him and touched him. He could see her quite clearly as a small, untidy little girl, dragging along behind Dick, a scruffy, adoring, little angel.

'I wish I could say "yes"!' She turned her sunbrown wistful face towards him, looking at him with honesty and liking, but without love. 'I do like you so very much, Phil. But I can't convince myself that liking is enough to make a marriage happy. I've thought about it a lot this last week. I think if it were only *my* future to be considered, I would say "yes". But there's yours, too, Phil. You may be quite sure now that it would be enough but I think as time went by you would want more from me than I could ever give you. I should find that instead of being able to make you happy, I was making you more and more frustrated and miserable. Don't ask me how I know this—it's just something that I feel deep down inside me.'

He gave a deep sigh. 'Perhaps you're right, Tamily. I have the idea that you very often are right. Maybe there is something in this "woman's intuition" after all. Maybe something will happen that none of us can foresee, and Dick will see you through my eyes. I wish I could make him, blast him! I sometimes wonder, listening to the pair of you, and knowing how you feel about him, how you can bear his casual, offhand affection. I know he's devoted to you in his own funny way. When you're not in the room he invariably says "Where's Tam?" It's almost as if he knew you as a kind of shadow without which like Peter Pan, he cannot be at ease. He is a kind of Peter Pan—the little boy who won't grow up. He may have the appearance of a man but he still has the heart of a boy.'

'Perhaps he always will!' Tamily said, surprised into this new understanding of Dick's nature. Phil's description fitted him so aptly. Was this the kind of man she really wanted? Someone whom she must look after, rather than someone to take care of her?

She shrugged her shoulders with a little gesture of despair. What use in surmising? There was no choice and, if there was, she would have Dick at any cost. Such is the price one has to pay for love.

SIXTEEN

'I don't believe it, I just don't believe!' Mercia was saying, over and over again. The news seemed to come to her with as much of a shock as it had hit Tamily when she'd opened the letter from Dick, earlier this cold November morning.

'I never thought it would come to anything serious,' Mercia went on. 'There must be some mistake, Tamily.'

For a moment, Tamily wondered whether she should have kept the news from Mercia of Dick's engagement to Anthea. But she realized that sooner or later, Mercia would have found out. Dick had written by the same post to his parents and there would have been no way to keep it from her indefinitely.

'Would you read me what he says?' Mercia was asking. 'There's nothing personal in the letter, is there?'

Tamily shook her head. She drew the envelope from the pocket of her slacks and spread the pages out on her knee as she sat hunched beside the cheerfully-blazing fire in Mercia's drawing-room. No matter how close she got to the fire, she could not seem to get warm and her hands holding the crumpled pages of Dick's letter were trembling.

'Darling Tammy,' she read aloud,

'I want you to be one of the first to hear my wonderful news. Anthea has agreed to marry me. I'm so incredibly happy I don't know how to begin to tell you about it. Of course, Phil knows and I think he'll come around to the idea once he's got over the shock! At present, he's mumbling about my being too young, and about sticking it out at Oxford until I've got my degree—generally being a bit of a wet blanket. Oddly enough, his objections don't seem to be that I'm not good enough for his sister, which I should have understood; he seems to think Anthea won't be the right wife for me. Why he imagines he knows better than I do what I want, heaven alone knows.

'I'm afraid Father might raise a few objections because I want to come down before I take my degree. I'd be awfully grateful, Tammy, if the opportunity arises, if you'd try to make him see that it will be much more valuable educationally to go

241

to Libya with Anthea and her father than to stay here and take a History degree that really won't be of any use to me later on.

'But I'm jumping ahead, aren't I? I haven't yet told you that we're planning to get married at the New Year and that the trip to Libya will be our honeymoon. I suppose there'll be plenty of people who think it odd having one's father-in-law on one's honeymoon, but as Anthea says, we shan't see much of him once he gets amongst the ruins and it will be a wonderfully romantic place for us.

'I haven't written to Mercia, as I feel rather badly about her. By that I mean that I know it will be a disappointment to her that I shan't be around when the baby arrives. So I leave it to you to tell her the best way you can, knowing that you'll find some way to break the news as kindly as possible.

'Of course, this means I shan't be home early next month as planned. I shall be going to London to stay with Anthea and her father and get my equipment sorted out for January. I will, of course, be home for Christmas—makes me sad to think it will be the last one we shall all have together.

'I have an idea that we shall be doing a lot of travelling in the future. I know Anthea

242

is anxious to go to New Guinea after Libya, so I shall probably be away from home quite a bit. I never thought Grandmother's money was going to come in so useful! She must have had a premonition that Mercia and I would marry so young and put in that clause about our coming into our legacies before we were twenty-one if we married. I expect Mercia's been finding it useful, too. Good old Grannie! She always did have a soft spot for us.

'It has only this minute occurred to me that those childish plans we made for farming Lower Beeches will now go by the board. However, I don't suppose you meant them any more seriously than I did although we did have fun talking about it, didn't we? In any case, I have an idea it won't be so long before you and Phil come together. Rather fun if you did, Tammy, because then we would be real brother and sister. I'd like this very much as it would keep us together in our old age, just as we've always been close in our childhood.

'Anthea and I have decided to have a quiet Register Office wedding. Anthea isn't a bit keen on all the paraphernalia of the church and it seems very sensible to me as she and her father want all their financial resources for the expedition. So long as we're really married, I can't see that it makes a

lot of difference although I shall never forget how beautiful Mercia looked on her wedding day, how moving the service was, and what fun it was afterwards at the reception.

'I suppose Mercia and Keith won't be able to come up for lunch after our wedding, but I hope you and Phil will come and of course Mother and Father. What about a "double" wedding, Tammy?—but perhaps that's more for a church do.

'I've rambled on long enough so I'll finish this off as I have still to write to Mother and Father. Incidentally, will you let me know in your next letter if you've started driving yet? I know you mentioned you might let Benson give you some lessons. If not, it would come in handy to have the Morris up here. I'm finding the train journeys to and from Anthea's at the week-ends a bit hard on the old bank balance and I reckon if I use a cheap grade of petrol I might save a few bob.

'Besides, the taxis in Town cost the earth and it'll mean I can travel back to Oxford much later on Sunday evenings. I think Father would let me have the Morris if I want it but I'll wait until I hear from you before I ask him.

'This is urgent, so write by return.

'Love as always, Dick.'

Tamily folded the letter and put it back in the envelope. For a moment the two girls sat in silence. Then Mercia said:

'I wouldn't mind if I thought she'd make him happy, but I can't think of anyone less suitable. Your Phil is right. They've nothing in common—she just isn't Dick's type. As for this expedition, can you see Dick taking up archaeology? I just don't understand it, Tamily.'

Tamily tried for the hundredth time to judge Anthea dispassionately; to remove the natural bias against any woman Dick found attractive and see her as another human being.

It was simple enough to understand that Dick should find her attractive. There was something so unusual and exotic in Anthea's appearance. That this mysteriousness had been carefully calculated, was neither here nor there. It was what lay beneath that mattered, and try though she might, Tamily could not envisage Anthea as a warm, loving person with the sole idea of making the man she married happy. She was always aloof, her face and eyes unanimated, unmoved except when she spoke of her one passion, archaeology.

Then only did she seem to come to life and a strange look of excitement would glow in those slanting brown eyes. They never glowed for Dick—or at least they never had during the fortnight they spent together here. Did she really love him? Somehow it seemed so much easier to think of Anthea crooning over some ancient Egyptian vase than warm and responsive in Dick's arms.

Yet Dick, although still so young, could not be completely blind. He must have seen another side to Anthea. Perhaps like many quiet and seemingly-emotionless people, there lurked beneath the surface a much more torrid passion than existed in the more extroverted type of woman. 'Still waters run deep'—Maybe she and Mercia knew nothing of the Anthea that Dick knew.

She tried hesitantly to convey these thoughts to Mercia, but Mercia would have none of it.

'I didn't like her. I never will. I don't believe she has the power to love. As for Dick, I don't believe he knows the meaning of the word, either. This is just a new craze for him, something unusual and exciting, that strikes him as being good fun. His letter proves it. It's not one long discourse of Anthea's charms as a man in love might be expected to write. It's the letter of a schoolboy, madly anxious to travel and see the world, excited by the novelty of it all.'

Deep in her heart, Tamily agreed. She had come straight to Mercia with the news, not waiting to hear Lord and Lady Allerton's reactions, and now as she sat wondering what they would say, she heard Lady Allerton's voice as she passed the drawing-room window.

She hurried to open the front door, for the rain was now pouring down and Lady Allerton must indeed be upset to have come down the long drive in this weather without even an umbrella to protect her from the rain. She hurried past Tamily and into the drawing-room, waving the letter from Dick in front of her.

'You've heard?' she questioned Mercia.

Mercia nodded.

'Something's got to be done. I'm not having Dick throwing himself away on a nobody. As for a Register Office wedding—I never heard of such a thing. And your father's quite hopeless! He says it's Dick's life and he refuses to withhold his consent. We've got to do something, Mercia. It's a most unsuitable marriage.'

She lowered her plump frame into the armchair beside her daughter, looking genuinely distressed. Mercia agreed that the marriage was unsuitable, but she was not prepared to go along with her mother as to the reasons.

'I don't see that it matters very much who Dick marries so long as he loves her and she loves him,' she said in her quiet, gentle voice. 'Perhaps Father is right—Dick is surely old enough to know what he's doing.'

'Rubbish!' Lady Allerton said sharply. 'He's only just nineteen. Of course he doesn't know what he wants. Libya! Expeditions! It's all a lot of ballyhoo. I'm going to write and tell Dick exactly what I think of him.'

Mercia sighed. She knew very well that her own marriage to Keith had been a disappointment. Lady Allerton would have preferred her to marry a title, but because she was the daughter it hadn't mattered so much. All her mother's hopes had been centred on Dick, who, it must be admitted, would one day have his father's title. Mercia understood her mother sufficiently well to realize that her preoccupation with society was the outcome of her own humble origins and might be excused on that score. Deep down, Lady Allerton was a kindly, affectionate woman and she had been remarkably nice about Keith and the coming baby, doing everything she could to assist the young couple.

'I don't know if family disapproval would be a deterrent to Dick if his mind is really made up,' Mercia said thoughtfully. 'I rather think it might have the effect of making him all the more determined. What do you think, Tamily?'

Tamily wasn't sure. Dick's love for his family was very deep-rooted and she sensed rather than knew that he would be bitterly unhappy if he thought there was going to be a permanent rift between them. The danger was that with his gay, optimistic nature, he would convince himself that they would not be angry with him for long and that by the time he returned from Libya they would be prepared to welcome both him and his bride with open arms. Lady Allerton had turned towards her, hopefully.

'Yes, Tamily. You've got some influence over Dick. Surely you can think of some way to stop this impossible marriage. Surely there's something you can think of that we could all do? If only I could persuade Dick's father to stop it. But he refuses to listen to me. He says we've no right to interfere or to put pressure on the boy.'

She forbore to mention that Lord Allerton had said:

'Don't forget, my dear, that we faced a deal of opposition before we could get married. Everyone thought it would be a mistake and yet we've been very happy together, haven't we?'

It was the first reference he had ever made to the fact that he took her out of the chorus and lifted her up beside him, proudly and affectionately, to take her place at his side. No one knew better than she how opposed his family were to the marriage, and she had understood the opposition. Richard's unwavering love and loyalty had overcome it in the end, just as she had overcome the difficulties in those early years when she was adapting herself to a new way of life.

She had less right than anyone to veto

Dick's choice. Not only had the gap between classes narrowed with the new Socialist outlook that followed upon the war, but there was a far less gap between Dick's social position and that of the girl he wanted to marry than had existed between herself and Lord Allerton, Anthea was clever, well-educated and came from a pleasant middle-class background. If only she could have *liked* the girl, she would not have felt so violently opposed to the match.

But Anthea, while always polite, had nevertheless managed to give Lady Allerton the feeling she hated most of all, inferiority. The girl would look at her with that aloof, calculating stare which made her remember she was not by birth the lady she had become. She had the impression that Anthea saw through the façade and despised her. No, she could never bring herself to like her. If this wedding took place, it would mean her darling Dick was lost for always. Why, she would have preferred him to have chosen a simple young girl like Tamily. She might lack position, money, brains, but at least Lady Allerton could have liked her.

'Perhaps he'll think better of it,' Tamily said helplessly, 'or maybe we are all quite wrong about Anthea and she truly loves Dick.'

'If she loved him, she wouldn't try and damage his career at Oxford,' Lady Allerton retorted sharply. 'Dick did very well with his intermediate and I've little doubt that he would get his degree in due course. Persuading him to go abroad with her has ruined all that. It's a pity your grandmother left you both her money,' she said, turning to Mercia. 'Gives you both far too much freedom. If Dick had to earn his living, he'd never be able to get away with this.'

Storm though she might, there was little that Lady Allerton or any of them could do. She and Mercia could write their disapproval to Dick, as indeed they did, but Tamily withheld her opinion. She could not believe it would affect Dick's decision; nor could she rid herself of the feeling that she was unjustly biased against the woman Dick professed to love. Her own letter she cut short saying simply that she had no need of the car and thanking Dick for considering her over the question of who should have it.

But she was not to get away with it so easily. A week later Dick wrote again, saying:

Were you just in a hurry or do you, too, disapprove? You all seem set against me, though why I simply cannot understand. You seemed to like Anthea last summer, so either you were merely being polite to her or else you are all against the idea of my marrying young. Surely YOU understand, Tammy. Do please sit down this minute and send me your congratulations. Thank heavens Father is being sensible. Very sporting in the circumstances, as he was a respectable forty when he made an honest woman of Mum.

I hate to think of Mercia being upset at a time like this. I never thought she'd take it this way, but her letter sounded very distressed and I would like to hear from you that she has become more accustomed to the idea now. Phil is being pig-headed and refuses to discuss the subject at all. So be on my side, please Tammy.

Ever your loving Dick.

Tamily wept hot, silent tears over the pages. It was true she'd always taken his

253

side but this time not even for his sake could she line up with him. How could he possibly expect her to be pleased? He must know that the plans they'd made to farm Lower Beeches had meant far more to her than a childish day-dream. She'd been so certain they'd meant more to Dick, too. Not only would all that be in the past, but Dick would be out of their lives in a way she had never envisaged even in her most pessimistic view of the future.

She wrote one reply after another and threw them all into the waste-paper basket, yet she could not answer him with silence. The letter she finally posted barely hid her true feelings:

Dearest Dick,

I'm afraid you've given us all rather a shock. Everyone knew you liked Anthea but nobody thought you would dream of getting married so suddenly. Perhaps we are all sorry to think that we shall be losing you and that no matter who the girl, we wouldn't have thought her good enough for you.

Naturally, you must act as your heart dictates, and if this is what you really want you know you have my very best wishes for your happiness.

Mercia hasn't been too well all week and perhaps this has depressed her unduly. There are only two months to go now and as it seems to be rather a large baby she's beginning to feel the strain. I don't think there is any cause for real worry but Mr Woods was here yesterday and reiterated rest, rest and more rest. Mercia is very obedient and Keith, of course, takes wonderful care of her.

We are all looking forward to seeing you at Christmas.

With love from
Tamily.

It was the best she could do but when Dick read it he was not satisfied.

Angrily, he threw the letter into the fire. To ease his troubled thoughts he went off to telephone Anthea. But there was no reassurance to be had from her, either. Anthea's father informed him, apologetically, that she had gone to a lecture on Ancient Greek Murals at the Victoria and Albert Museum. He told his prospective father-in-law not to bother to ask Anthea to ring him back.

SEVENTEEN

Fortunately, Keith was home for lunch when Mercia's baby started to arrive. Tamily was washing up when Keith called her quickly from the kitchen. He looked white-faced and anxious.

'Run up to the Manor quickly,' he ordered her. 'I think the baby's on the way. Tell Benson to come back with the Morris. He may have to go and fetch Sister Weatherby if there's no quick train; and tell them to put bottles in the bed as I'll be bringing Mercia up in about ten minutes. I must get on to Dr Timms first.'

Tamily stared back at him anxiously.

'But, Keith, the Morris isn't there. Dick's got it, and I know Lord Allerton took the Rolls to Westminster this morning.'

'Then Benson will have to drive my car,' Keith retorted.

Obediently, Tamily ran out of the house, heedless of the rain on her bare head, and arrived soaked and breathless at the Manor. She dashed in through the garden door and nearly knocked over her mother. She gasped out the news and said: 'Benson *is* here, isn't he? He's back?'

Jess shook her head. 'He hasn't arrived yet. He left about seven o'clock. He reckoned it would take him about two hours to get to Oxford, then I suppose it would be another hour by train back to London. I don't quite see how he could get here much before tea.'

Tamily tried to remain cool. It wasn't so important. If the maternity nurse who had been engaged for the confinement could come by train, there was always a taxi from the station.

The thought suddenly stuck her that perhaps Sister Weatherby might not be available. She'd been engaged for early February and the chances were she'd be away still on an earlier case.

She tore back to the Dower House and found Keith kneeling beside Mercia, holding her hand, one eye on his watch.

'The pains are coming at twenty-minute intervals,' he said, in his calm, professional voice. 'The baby won't arrive just yet.'

Mercia opened her eyes, and smiled up at him.

'Stop worrying, darling,' she said. 'Surely

you as a doctor know that thousands of seven-month babies arrive without any trouble at all. You ought to be pleased for me that I'm not going to have to wait another eight weeks, after all.'

Keith motioned to Tamily to leave the room, and followed her quickly into the hall.

'Whatever you do, don't let Mercia see you're worried,' he told her. 'But everything seems to be going wrong. Dr Timms is on another maternity case which nurse says he can't leave as there's the possibility of a breech-birth. And Sister Weatherby isn't at home. The woman she shares a flat with has given me the address of her present patient but can't tell me whether she'll be able to leave even for an emergency. I've booked the call—it's only about twenty miles from here. If she can only manage to come. Benson can go off straight away for her.'

Unhappily, Tamily told him the Benson wasn't here. Before Keith could reply, the telephone shrilled suddenly, and he rushed to answer it. He listened attentively for a few minutes and then said briefly:

'Someone will fetch you, Sister, in about half an hour. Thanks a lot. Will you thank your patient for me?'

He turned to Tamily with a look of relief.

'It's all right,' he told her. 'Sister Weatherby's patient is releasing her. The baby's a fortnight old and doing well and the mother is up and about, so they don't mind at all. Sister Weatherby is the best maternity nurse there is and Mr Woods swears by her. I shall go for her myself, Tamily, as soon as we've got Mercia up to the Manor. The District Nurse should be here in a few minutes and Dr Timms will, I hope, be up long before the baby arrives.'

Tamily looked at him anxiously.

'How long will that be?'

Keith frowned.

'It's hard to say exactly. Certainly not for several hours. I shall be back with Sister Weatherby in plenty of time.'

They went back into Mercia's bedroom and she gave them a wan smile of welcome. Keith went over to her and held her hand tightly.

'Everything's going to be all right, darling,' he said reassuringly. 'The District Nurse will be here directly and I'm going over to fetch Sister Weatherby. By a piece of good fortune, she's with a patient only a short distance away.'

A look of distress clouded Mercia's white face.

'Oh, Keith, do you have to go?'

And then she forced a smile and said quickly:

'Of course, you wouldn't be leaving me unless it was necessary. But come back quickly.'

They waited until the next pain had passed and then Keith wrapped her warmly in several blankets and with Tamily's help assisted her into his car. Jess was waiting at the front door and between them they carried Mercia up to the old nursery wing which had been prepared well in advance for the coming baby. It had been thought advisable for Mercia to be in the Manor rather than her own home, as there were plenty of people to look after her and the baby and the maternity nurse. The nursery suite consisted of four light, airy rooms, of which one had been prepared for the baby's delivery and it was here they brought Mercia.

Keith disappeared and returned in a few moments with a glass, which he explained to Mercia contained something to make her sleep.

'By the time you come to, I'll be back,' he said and as soon as she had drunk it obediently he turned and hurried away.

Tamily sat by the bed, holding Mercia's hand. She felt frightened by the unexpected turn of events, frightened for Mercia. But Keith's calm organization had been reassuring and obviously there were no complications expected, or he would have had Mercia sent straight to the nearest hospital. She was not to know that he had already telephoned the hospital, asking for an incubator to be sent for the baby, who would now be premature. He was leaving nothing to chance.

Mercia was not yet asleep, but in the draught Keith had given her was a strong tranquillizer and she seemed very calm.

'Just think, Tamily, by this evening my baby will be born. I shall know whether I've succeeded in giving Keith his son. It's very exciting, isn't it?'

Tamily nodded. She could understand Mercia's impatience to put the long wait behind her and to hold the baby in her arms.

'Is everything ready?' Mercia asked drowsily.

Again Tamily nodded. Not far from the

bed a table stood covered with a clean white sheet and laden with all the items that could possibly be needed for the baby's delivery. Tamily and her mother had been wise to do this so well in advance. When Jess had received Tamily's message, she had only to spread a sheet on the table and lay out the paraphernalia. Apart from the chair on which Tamily sat, the room was bare and the lino floor had been scrubbed clean. It might have been a hospital ward, smelling slightly of disinfectant and, according to Keith, who had inspected it, now the ideal labour room.

Mercia seemed to drift into a shallow sleep. Once or twice she moaned slightly, but she did not stir, even when Jess came in with the District Nurse and a tray of tea-things.

Tamily and the young nurse talked in whispers. Tamily rather liked the girl and was reassured by her statement that the next baby would make the total she had delivered nearly a century.

'Perhaps I'll be able to stay and help Sister Weatherby,' she said to Tamily, hopefully. 'Although my experience of maternity nurses is that they are very possessive with their patients.'

Tamily put the tea-tray outside the door, and going back into the room, glanced at her watch. Keith had been gone nearly two hours. Surely he should be back by now! Perhaps he had called in at the hospital, for something Sister wanted; perhaps Sister had not been ready, or was he trying to get hold of Dr Timms, who had still not arrived? Mercia was awake now and the nurse came over to Tamily and whispered:

'She's been asking for her husband. The pains are coming quite frequently now.'

'I'll go and see if Dr Parker has returned,' Tamily said anxiously.

Downstairs, the large house seemed quite deserted. Lady Allerton had gone to Town with her husband for a day's shopping and the only person to be seen was Simmonds, polishing the dining-room silver. She hurried past him into the kitchen to find Jess and Cook discussing the evening meal. They looked up as she came in and asked after Mercia.

'She's all right,' Tamily said, 'but Nurse seems to think the baby might be coming fairly soon. I can't think what's happened to Keith. He reckoned it would only take him an hour and a half, at the most.'

She tried not to worry but she felt strangely perturbed. Perhaps the darkening light of the late November afternoon had something to do with it. Outside the rain still poured down in steady sheets and the quiet unnerved her. She went slowly back upstairs, unwilling to have to tell Mercia that Keith had not yet returned. As she opened the door, Nurse hurried over to her.

'This baby's in a nice hurry to make its way into the world. Good thing I brought my gas and air. You'd better get scrubbed up and put on that green overall,' she continued. 'I may need some help.'

Quite suddenly Tamily's fear was gone. She felt a strange excitement at the thought that she might be able to help in this great miracle of birth. She wished she'd had more knowledge of the subject. But at least she'd watched the foals being born, and had been there when Dick's spaniel's puppies had arrived. She wasn't entirely ignorant of what she might expect.

Quietly, efficiently, she obeyed the Nurse's orders as if she had been doing this kind of work all her life. The gas and air seemed to bring Mercia relief from the worst of the pain, but every now and again she would cling to Tamily's hand, her eyes closed tightly, her forehead bathed in sweat, and she would call for Keith.

'He'll be here presently,' Tamily said again and again. But as the minutes ticked by and another half-hour passed, she became seriously worried. If something had gone wrong with the car, why couldn't he have telephoned? He must himself be desperately anxious about Mercia. What could have happened?

Five minutes later, Dr Timms arrived. He gave Mercia a quick inspection and hurried Tamily out of the room.

'You've got to prepare yourself for some bad news, Tamily,' he told her immediately the door closed behind them. 'There's been an accident.'

Tamily stared at him, aghast.

'Not—not Keith?'

The old doctor nodded his head.

'The police got in touch with me half an hour ago. It seems the car skidded on the wet road and another car coming in the opposite direction hit them head-on.'

'How terrible!' Tamily breathed. 'Was Sister Weatherby with him? Are they both hurt? Have they been taken to hospital?'

Dr Timms took her hand and held it tightly.

'I'm afraid it's worse than that, my dear,' he told her gently. 'They were both killed instantly.'

For a moment the shock numbed all feeling. With surprise, Tamily felt that she had known all along this was going to happen. It was as if Dr Timms had merely confirmed something that, deep down inside, she already knew. Then full realization of what had happened flooded over her.

'Mercia!'

She stared up at Dr Timms, as if he could perform some miracle and make this horrible nightmare untrue.

'She mustn't be told, not on any account. Let her go on believing all is well for a little while longer. She must have her baby in peace.'

The door opened suddenly behind them and the nurse's voice said sharply: 'It's coming, Doctor!'

She hurried back to her patient. Dr Timms followed her. This time Tamily could not go with them. Not even the knowledge that Mercia's baby was about to be born could rouse her from the deep shock of numbness that seemed to hold her body immobile.

There was the sense of personal loss. Keith, who was so kind and good, so terribly young to die. He would never now know the child Mercia had wanted so much to give him. And Mercia—the tragedy that this would mean in her life was too terrible to take in fully. Perhaps the baby would bring her some consolation, and yet Tamily knew deep down in her heart that Mercia hadn't wanted the baby for herself; she had wanted it for Keith.

There was a sudden flurry of noise in the downstairs hall, and Tamily heard Lady Allerton's rather strident voice calling her.

Slowly she descended the stairs and Lady Allerton ran forward, her face bright with happy excitement.

'Simmonds just told me. Isn't it thrilling! The baby hasn't come yet, has it? Mercia's all right?'

'So she doesn't know,' Tamily thought, striving to keep calm. 'But then, how could she?'

Lord Allerton was smiling.

'Just think—a grandchild! It hardly seemed real until now. I must go and speak to Simmonds about the champagne.

If it's a boy, we must put down a good cellar for him.'

'Stop it!' Tamily broke in, suddenly unable to bear their happiness. She didn't know, but there were tears running down her cheeks and Lord and Lady Allerton were staring at her, shocked and anxious now.

'What's happened?' Lady Allerton asked sharply, and taking Tamily's arms she shook the girl in her impatience. 'Mercia's all right, isn't she? Speak up, child!'

Tamily gently detached her arms from Lady Allerton's grasp and clenched her hands to her sides.

'It's Keith,' she said staringly. 'He went to fetch Sister Weatherby and on the way back the car skidded. They're both dead.'

Their faces stared at her, wiped clean of happiness now, and she watched curiously as realization of what this must mean to their daughter twisted their features to a grimace.

'I must go to her, my poor darling!' Lady Allerton cried, breaking the appalling silence.

But Tamily shook her head. 'She doesn't know—Dr Timms says no one must tell her.'

She saw Lord Allerton put an arm round his wife's shoulders and lead her gently into the drawing-room. Tamily felt suddenly desperately alone. She went slowly back up the stairs, trying to find some happy consolation in the thought that Keith's child was about to enter the world. But before she reached the top landing, she was halted by a thin, querulous wail. Tamily sat down on the top stair and buried her face in her arms.

EIGHTEEN

It was nearly midnight. Tamily felt completely and utterly exhausted. Behind her in the darkened room the night nurse, whom Dr Timms had managed miraculously to find, was sitting by Mercia's bed, her eyes never leaving her patient's face. A long snaking tube hung from a cylinder above the bed and disappeared into Mercia's smooth, white arm. Minute by minute the blood that would help to make Mercia strong again was dripping into her veins. She would get well, strong; she must.

But Tamily knew that Dr Timms was greatly worried. The birth had been uncomplicated, but the haemorrhages which followed had had a terrible effect upon Mercia. Tamily knew that it was only thanks to Dr Timms's skill and the level-headed efficiency of the young District Nurse that Mercia was alive now. They had worked tirelessly stopping the first haemorrhage with injections, only a little while later to be faced with another.

Dr Timms was away now collecting another bottle of plasma from the hospital. Tamily marvelled at the old man's stamina. She knew he'd been up most of the night before with his previous case and he'd had no rest. What had undermined all of them was Mercia's ceaseless demand for Keith. She would rouse from unconsciousness and her voice would reiterate over and over again:

'Where's Keith? Could somebody find Keith? Please, Tamily, could you fetch Keith?'

She had not asked about her baby. She had not even inquired if it were a boy or a girl. Perhaps it was as well, Tamily thought, for Mercia hadn't managed to

270

produce the son she had wanted. The tiny baby lying in the incubator in the next room, swathed in cotton-wool, was a little girl. Surprisingly for a premature baby, she weighed $5\frac{1}{2}$ pounds, and was not in the least ugly. There was even a fluff of fair hair on the tiny head and as Tamily had bent over to take her first look, the baby had opened eyes as blue as Dick's and Mercia's.

Her heart had gone out to the small morsel of humanity and she had longed to pick it up in her arms and cradle it.

Her eyes felt heavy with fatigue, but although the night nurse had suggested repeatedly that she should go and get some sleep, Tamily could not bring herself to leave Mercia's side. In her moments of consciousness, Mercia's eyes would search the room for Tamily as if she were a link with Keith, she alone able to bring him to her. It was an agonizing responsibility, knowing that Mercia trusted her as she lied over and over again, giving one excuse after another why Keith had been delayed. She wondered just how convincing those lies had been. Had there been doubt in those eyes? Certainly there had been fear. It depended how drugged she really was.

If her mind had been fully alert, Mercia must have known that Keith would have let nothing stand between him and his wife at such a time; no puncture or breakdown would have deterred him. He'd have been here even if he had to walk the twenty miles.

Tamily had used instead the more credible lie that Keith had been called to an emergency case. Mercia knew how conscientious Keith always was with his patients and at first this lie had seemed to satisfy her. But as the night wore on, there had been no look of reassurance in her eyes. She had continued to stare at Tamily silently and with what Tamily felt sure was doubt.

With a sense of relief, Tamily heard Dr Timms on the landing and the night nurse went out of the room to meet him. As the door closed quietly behind her, Tamily heard Mercia call her name. She went quickly to the bed and took Mercia's hand in hers. Quite distinctly, Mercia said: 'Has something happened to Keith? Please tell me the truth, Tammy.'

Her hesitation lasted only a fraction of a second, but even as the new lie formed on her lips, Mercia interrupted her.

'I want the truth, darling. I know something is wrong. I know you're trying to keep it from me. Don't you see, *I've got to know!* I shan't be able to rest until I do know, and I'm so tired.'

Dr Timms had come into the room and heard Mercia's voice. As Tamily looked up, question in her eyes, he nodded his head resignedly. The worry of doubt was doing as much harm as the truth could do. They must somehow put her mind at rest, with a half-truth, maybe. He went himself to Mercia's bed and said:

'I'm afraid he's been in an accident, Mercia. He's in hospital and that's why he can't be here with you. He's in no pain and in the very best of care. You cannot help him by worrying about him, and you know, if he were here now he would want you to do as I tell you and rest. I'm going to give you an injection to make you sleep, and when you wake I'll answer all your questions.'

If the news had been a shock to her, she gave no sign of it. She listened to Dr Timms quietly and when he'd finished she turned her head away from him and closed her eyes. She did not open them even when the hypodermic pricked her skin. Dr Timms turned to Tamily:

'You ought to go to bed now,' he ordered her. 'She won't awaken before morning and there's nothing you can do.'

But Tamily waited until the injection had taken effect and she knew that Mercia was sleeping, then with a last request to the night nurse to call her the moment Mercia woke, she went obediently to her room.

Exhaustion, combined with the nervous strain of this terrible day, had its effect. As she drifted towards sleep, she remembered that nobody had thought to inform Dick. She wondered if he would still be at Oxford. His last letter had not given the exact date he would leave for London. She tried to remember if they had Anthea's telephone number, but before she could puzzle it out sleep overcame her.

The morning broke late with another cold, grey, November day. The rain had ceased but a heavy wet mist hung about the air, damp and uninviting. Tamily dressed quickly and drank the hot tea Jess had brought to her with the message that Mercia was awake and asking for her.

As she went into the room, Tamily was shocked to see that Dr Timms was still there. He looked dishevelled and utterly worn out. He drew Tamily aside and told her that he had sent for Mr Woods.

'I'm afraid she had another haemorrhage in the night, and she's very weak,' he said in an undertone. 'I'm not at all happy about her. I'm quite convinced there's nothing organically wrong. The confinement was absolutely straightforward. It may be just shock and loss of blood, but I can't help feeling uneasy. It's almost as if she knows what has happened and she's deliberately willing herself to go with him: I had nurse bring the baby to her, although it shouldn't have been brought out of the incubator. I hoped it might rouse her a little from this apathy. But she wouldn't even look at it, and that's unusual, you know. The maternal instinct is so strong in a woman that her child's cry can nearly always make her forget everything else. Woods should be here in an hour. Meanwhile, Tamily, do what you can for her. Lie as much as you have to. Say you've rung the hospital and heard he's doing fine—anything you like, but don't let her realize she'll never see him again.'

Tamily was shocked by the pallor of Mercia's face. There was not the slightest trace of colour in it and her skin was waxen. The eyes that stared up at Tamily seemed vast in that thin, drawn little face. She tried and succeeded to hide her own fear and distress and smiled brightly at Mercia.

'Keith's fine, darling!' she said, cheerfully. 'They reckon he'll be out of hospital in a day or two. The ward sister said he was thrilled to bits to hear about the baby. He sent you his fondest love.'

There was no answering smile, not even a change in the expressionless face.

'Have you any message for him?' Tamily persisted.

With horror, she saw two tears cloud the blue eyes and roll down Mercia's cheeks. Then Mercia spoke: 'Tammy, I want to talk to you alone. Can you ask the others to go?'

Dr Timms had heard the quiet voice. He gave a warning look at Tamily and then beckoned the nurse to follow him out of the door. Mercia reached for Tamily's hand and held it in a surprisingly strong grip.

'I know!' she whispered. 'You're all trying to keep it from me, but I know. He's dead, isn't he.'

Tamily drew in her breath sharply. The

last sentence had not been a question; it had been a statement of fact.

'It's no good lying to me any more, darling,' Mercia said gently. 'You don't do it very well. I think I knew the moment it actually happened. I want you to understand, Tammy—the others might not. I don't want to go on living in a world where there's no Keith. I'm not going to try to get well and strong. Wherever Keith is now, I want to be with him.'

Tamily knelt by the bed and took Mercia's hands in her own, holding them tightly as if she could will her own health and strength into the other girl.

'You mustn't talk like that, Mercia,' she cried urgently. 'There's the baby—you've got to get well. Keith would want you to go on living—I know he would.'

Mercia shook her head. 'But *I* don't want to,' she said, the words strangely final. 'You can have my baby, Tammy. I'd like you to have it. You'll be a wonderful mother. I'm leaving it in your care, darling.'

Tamily was so distressed, for a moment she could not speak. Then she said: 'You don't really mean this, Mercia. It's just because of all the drugs you've had. You'll feel quite differently in a little while. I'm not going to listen to you saying these awful things.'

Mercia turned her head restlessly on the pillow.

'Please, Tammy,' she said. 'They'll be back in a minute and I do so want *you* to understand. I don't want you to grieve for me. Can't you see that this is my only chance of happiness now, and I'm not sorry it's all turned out this way. I'm not even sad about Keith. We've been so wonderfully happy together. I don't think life could offer any more than we had. I don't think that kind of perfection can last the normal span of a lifetime. I might have got ill, been a handicap to Keith. He might have had to make sacrifices for me, curtail his ambitions. I think I would have been desperately unhappy if such a thing had occurred. This way, we've known all that's best in life and there was never anything but harmony between us. Let me go to him, Tammy. Don't try to hold me back with your grief.'

Dr Timms and the nurse came back into the room. Tamily didn't know it, but the door had been ajar and he had deliberately overheard the conversation. He knew now what he was up against and realized that he had been justifiably afraid. This kind of illness was not listed in his medical dictionaries. There was no such disease as that of a broken heart. Yet, he had come across it before, in women who had lost their children, in husbands who had lost dearly-loved wives. He knew, too, that it sprang from deeply primeval emotions. One came across it in uncivilized tribes where a man had been known to take to his bed in the prime of physical perfection and mentally killed himself in a matter of weeks, to fade to a mere skeleton and die. In such cases, post-mortems found nothing wrong and these deaths remained a mystery.

He had brought Mercia into the world eighteen years ago and could not bring himself to relinquish her without a fight. There was nothing the specialist could do when he came and little he could do himself. But like Tamily, he never left Mercia's bedside, and whenever she was conscious he argued with her fiercely, trying to instil in her the will to live.

It was no use. Tamily was forced to realize this when evening came and a white-faced, shocked Dick knelt by Mercia's bed, and begged her to get well again. Mercia's only reply was a tiny shake of the head. Not even for Dick, her adored brother, would she make the effort.

Dick was distraught. He had always adored the golden-haired little girl, always protected her and given her all that was best in himself. For someone as full of health and energy as he had always been, one might have supposed that illness would be alien to him. One would have excused a schoolboy for avoiding the sick-room, and yet he had never been far from it.

Now he seemed unable to stand the atmosphere of the room where Mercia lay. He hung around the door, pacing the length of the landing, restless, desperately unhappy. After his one brief conversation with his sister, he seemed to accept that nothing he could say would bring a smile back to her eyes or the colour to her cheeks. Yet he was not willing to accept what this would mean. He made frantic suggestions to Tamily.

'Can't we get another specialist? Surely there must be something we can do? We can't just stand by and watch her die, Tamily?'

He seemed completely preoccupied with

the thought of saving her and it was not until late that night, when Dr Timms had warned them that she might not last until morning, that it suddenly occurred to Dick that he was responsible. He took Tamily into the old schoolroom adjoining the nursery suite and held her arms so tightly that she was conscious of pain.

'It's all my fault!' He all but shouted the words at her. 'Don't you see, Tammy, that if it hadn't been for me, this would never have happened?'

Tamily tried to force her tired brain to follow his reasoning. She couldn't see how he could possibly have arrived at such a conclusion. He released her arm and strode to and fro as if he could not bear his own thoughts.

'You said Benson couldn't go for the nurse because he hadn't got back from Oxford. If I hadn't sent for the car when I did, Benson would have gone for her, not Keith. Then he'd be here—Keith would be here. Oh my God, Tammy, I can't stand it.'

He sat down suddenly on the worn chintz window-seat and buried his face in his hands. Appalled, she saw his shoulders shaking and heard the harsh, tortured sobs.

Dick—Dick who never cried, even as a small boy when he'd fallen through the greenhouse roof and cut his arm so badly he had to have twelve stitches. She went over and knelt beside him, not daring to touch him but near enough for him to know she was there.

'That's crazy, Dick,' she said firmly and authoritatively. 'It's the most far-fetched idea I've ever heard. Of course it wasn't your fault. If you want to take it to its logical conclusion, you might blame Benson. He stopped for coffee at Paddington and missed the train from Victoria. If he hadn't wanted coffee, he'd have been back here in time.'

But he seemed not to hear her. She heard his voice, muffled by his hands.

'I'll never forgive myself if she dies.'

She wanted to be able to tell him that Mercia was going to be all right. She would have given her own life for that moment in exchange. But she knew, just as Dr Timms, the nurse, Dick, that Mercia was growing weaker and that it was only a matter of time. She tried to comfort him with Mercia's own words of comfort to her.

'She doesn't want to go on living in a

world where there's no Keith—she doesn't want to get better. At first I wanted to fight against it, too. But I'm not sure any more, Dick. Maybe she is right. Maybe she wouldn't be able to find happiness without Keith. She loved him so much. Perhaps it's selfish of us to want to keep her with us.'

He seemed unconscious of his wild, tortured expression as he stared up at her.

'You can't mean that, Tammy? You can't want her to die.'

'No, no, of course I don't!' Tamily said in a low voice. 'But it's what *she* wants, Dick.'

He seemed not to understand what she was trying to tell him and desperately she fought for some way to make him see.

'Suppose it were you, Dick. You're in love with Anthea. Imagine that you've just heard she had died. Would you feel like going on living? Wouldn't it seem to you that death was a happy release from a world without her?'

Dick was frowning, his face as perplexed as before. 'No, of course it wouldn't. There are other things to live for besides love. I can't understand you talking about things like this, Tammy. I can only think the strain's been a bit much for you. Of course I love Anthea; of course it would be a ghastly shock, but as for wanting to end my own life, what possible purpose could that serve?'

'It wouldn't serve any purpose at all,' Tamily argued desperately. 'I'm just trying to make you understand that it's what you might want to do. If you loved her as much as Mercia loved Keith, you couldn't envisage life as a happy place if she were gone.'

If nothing else, the conversation seemed to have helped Dick recover his composure. He stood up, shrugging his shoulders, and pushing the brown curly hair away from his forehead.

'Then I guess I just don't love her as much,' he admitted. 'Don't you see, Tammy, that even if there were no Anthea, there'd be lots of other things worth living for. There'd be you, Mercia, the farm. Why, I'd probably go back to my old plan of farming Lower Beeches with you. It would be a full and a satisfying life. As for Mercia, she's got Keith's child. Isn't that a reason for her to want to live? You're wrong, Tammy, and I'm going to make

Mercia realize that she's wrong, too.'

She was too tired to make the effort to stop him as he strode determinedly out of the room. She sat down on the chair he had vacated and laid her head back, closing her eyes wearily. Mercia had been afraid the others wouldn't understand. But Tamily understood. She knew how pointless life would seem without Dick, and hers was a love that was not required, as Mercia's had been. To have known Dick's love and to have lost it, that indeed would be the end of her world. She was startled by the sound of footsteps in the room. She opened her eyes and saw Dick standing there. He looked stunned.

'It's no use, Tammy.' The words were devoid of the earlier emotion. 'It's too late, she's gone.'

NINETEEN

Tamily sat in the nursery listening to the cheerful 'hiss' of the gas-fire. In front of it a row of clean muslin nappies were airing and the room smelt of a mixture of talcum powder and drying clothes. It was warm, comfortable, cosy, in the way that only a nursery can be.

Tamily thought gratefully that she was lucky to be here. Somehow, she did not think she could have borne to attend Keith's and Mercia's funeral.

The house was empty. Everyone, including all the servants, had gone to pay their last respects with the family mourners. This morning, Jess had taken charge of the baby while Tamily went down to the church to decorate it once again with a mass of white flowers. When she had left, the dark and rather gloomy interior had been brightened by the beautiful vases of white chrysanthemums, the tall stately lilies, and simple michaelmas daisies.

She was reminded sharply that it wasn't yet a year since she had last decorated this church for Mercia's marriage. She was beyond tears. The enormity of the double tragedy had shocked the whole household into a numb despair. The village, too, had been appalled. Messages from all the simple folk who had known Mercia all her life poured in together with the flowers, telegrams and wreaths from the family's acquaintances. Amidst the general sorrow, everyone seemed to have forgotten Mercia's baby. Tamily looked tenderly at the tiny girl. How like Mercia she seemed! The incubator had been returned to the hospital for although premature, the baby had progressed steadily, and except for the extra care of bathing her tender skin with olive oil instead of soap and water, and for giving her three-hourly instead of four-hourly feeds, Dr Timms had pronounced her perfectly well able to be treated as a normal, full-term child.

Lady Allerton had wanted to call in another maternity nurse but Tamily had begged to be allowed to look after the baby herself. She'd had no experience with young babies, and at first even Dr Timms had been doubtful as to the advisability of leaving so young a baby in inexperienced hands. But Tamily's calm efficiency with the child, the quick easy way in which she learned from the hospital nurse and the District Nurse, convinced him that here was a born mother. Dr Timms knew, perhaps better than anyone else, just how deeply Tamily was grieving for Mercia. To let her have the responsibility of the child would take her mind off herself. He knew that the District Nurse would be calling twice a day and he, himself, would be within call should any emergency arise. Jess, too, was a sensible and capable woman, well able to share the task with Tamily. Lady Allerton had given way with surprising ease. She seemed too wrapped up in her grief to care greatly one way or the other. She had referred the matter to her husband and the old gentleman had shaken his head sadly and said:

'If Dr Timms says it's all right, my dear, why not?'

'They don't really care about her,' thought Tamily. 'I'm the only one who really loves her. She's mine now. Mercia gave her to me.'

She felt a fierce, possessive love well up in her. No one else might care but she loved the baby, no harm should ever come to her. She was going to spend the rest of her life seeing that she was well and happy and all that Mercia would have wished her to be. In her mind, she had already christened the baby Mercia. She bore such a marked resemblance to her mother that it both hurt and pleased Tamily to look in those blue eyes.

The clock ticked slowly on towards the hour. Presently they would come back and it would all be over. She tried not to think of the ghastly preparations of the last days. There had been the inquest on Keith, which Dick and Lord Allerton had to attend; the relatives of Sister Weatherby to be written to; Insurance Companies to be notified. The police were at the Manor questioning everyone. Mercifully, no blame was attached to Keith for the accident. Although he had been driving fast, the man in the other car, who was only slightly injured, had testified at the inquest that Keith was well on his own side of the road and must have struck a greasy patch to have skidded in the way he did. Lord Allerton had promised generous compensation to Sister Weatherby's relatives, in addition to anything the Insurance Companies would eventually be doing for them.

Tamily dared not think about the funeral. To keep her mind from remembering, she tried to think coolly and sensibly about the future. Soon Dick would be gone and she would settle down to a life at the Manor with the baby. In a way, it was a kind of miracle. She had thought she would no longer be needed by the family, and here was a greater need than ever before. It was almost as if her destiny had been planned beforehand. There was no longer the slightest doubt in her mind that she could never marry Phil. She loved Dick, for better or for worse, as Mercia had loved Keith. And since this could never be now, how lucky she was to have someone else to live for; someone else to need her!

It gave her a sense of security she had not known for over a year. Not only was this Mercia's child, but it was related also to Dick and the family likeness was there in the eyes, just as it had existed between brother and sister. It was one small tie with him which could never be severed.

Perhaps Fate had decided to deal with her kindly in the end. Had this been the boy that Mercia had longed for, he would have needed a father far more than did a little girl.

So she consoled herself, little knowing that her plans were laid on foundations that would collapse beneath her feet! And it was Dick, of all people, who was to sweep all her new-found peace of mind away with the cruel words which were his first remark when he returned from the funeral.

'Of course Mercia's child is not going to know it has lost both father and mother.

Anthea and I will bring it up as our own.'

Tamily took an involuntary step towards the baby's cot and grasped the muslin frilled edge possessively.

'But Dick, Mercia gave her to me. She's mine now. You can't take her away.'

Dick looked surprised.

'But Tammy, you can't possibly bring up a child on your own.' His tone was kindly, but his words cut her heart as if they had been deliberately aimed. 'She's got to have the very best.'

She was stung to reply: 'And you think *you* can give it to her, you and Anthea? Do you think either of you can love her more than I do? Mercia wanted *me* to have her. She knew I would devote my whole life to her.'

Dick was staring at her across the room. The gulf between them seemed to be widening with every moment that passed. It had never been like this before. No matter how fiercely they argued, they had somehow always remained close. He was suddenly a stranger, someone who was trying to take her child away.

'But she's not yours,' Dick said sharply. 'She's not even related to you. I'm her uncle, and it's only right that I should have charge of her.'

Tamily sat down again weakly and stared into the steady flame of the gas-fire.

'I can't see why you want her, Dick. You can't trail a baby across Libyan deserts. She'd mean nothing to Anthea. You don't even know if Anthea would be willing to adopt her.'

Dick strode over to the cot and stared down at the baby. The likeness to its mother struck him as forcibly as it had done Tamily, a short while ago. He had never been so wretchedly unhappy in his whole life. Down there, in the churchyard, they had put Mercia into the cold ground, and he had felt as if part of him had gone with her. He knew he would never be young again. Childhood was really gone now, along with Mercia. But here in the cot lay his one chance to make amends. For the rest of his life he would feel responsible for his sister's death. If he could only have her baby, perhaps he could atone for his wretched selfishness. But Tamily, of all people, was standing in his way and she had struck home with that last remark. How could they trail the baby into the Libyan desert? If they left

292

it behind this time, what about the New Guinea expedition Anthea was planning for next year?

Perhaps he could persuade Anthea to give up the idea of travelling round the world. Perhaps she would be willing to settle down and bring up a family. But even as the hope sprang to his mind, it was followed closely by the certainty that nothing would deviate Anthea from the path she had mapped for herself. He'd known before their engagement that he must marry into her world; not, as was customary, she into his. It hadn't seemed to matter at the time. It had all sounded rather fun and he had felt sure that he would have enjoyed it. He could still have enjoyed it were it not for the baby.

His own uncertainty made him speak more firmly.

'Of course Anthea will be willing to adopt the child. When she knows what it means to me, she will be just as willing as I am to sacrifice her plans.'

Tamily swung round, her eyes blazing.

'Sacrifice!' she echoed. 'Do you think that kind of love is what a child needs? It would grow up knowing that Anthea resented her for coming between her and her ambitions. She would blame you, too, Dick. The baby would be a sort of contention between you. Why can't you let me have her? I've nothing else, Dick.'

'Because I can't!' Dick flung at her. 'I've got to have her, Tamily. Don't you see that this is the only way I can make up to Mercia for doing her out of all those years of happiness to which she was entitled?'

Tamily's face lost all vestige of colour. At last she understood. It wasn't the baby Dick wanted, it was a chance to rid himself of that terrible feeling of guilt with which he was scourging himself, despite all their efforts to make him see he could not be held responsible.

She was torn in two. Going once more to the cot she looked down at the tiny, sleeping figure with deep longing. They could have been so happy, the two of them. Tamily would have loved her so very, very much. But she knew she would never now know a moment's peace of mind with that look in Dick's eyes haunting her. There was no one else in the whole world to whom she would have relinquished her right to the baby but she knew she was helpless, as always, in the face of her love for him.

'All right, Dick,' she said quietly. 'If Anthea is willing to adopt her, I won't stand in your way.'

He made a movement towards her but she went quickly past him, unable to bear the sound of his gratitude. She knew she would never go near the baby again. Until Dick took it with him, it must have a nurse after all. Or Jess must care for it. She, herself, was too weak to trust herself to hold the baby in her arms again.

Next time she might not be able to put Dick first.

She went to her room and lay, dry-eyed, on the bed...

Anthea came forward to meet him, her usually calm face softened for once with sympathy.

'Poor darling!' she said, leading Dick to a comfortable wing chair by the fire. 'You look perfectly ghastly. Let me get you a drink.'

He shook his head, impatiently. He had caught the first train to London and rushed here in a taxi, knowing he could not relax until he had put the most important question to her. He was encouraged by her gentleness, the sympathy that showed clearly in her voice and manner.

Impulsively, he plunged into his account of what had happened, giving her no warning, no time to prepare herself as he ended his explanation, saying:

'You agree with me, don't you darling, that we should take the baby? Tamily has promised not to try to prevent us. Strictly speaking, I suppose Mother and Father are its legal guardians, but Mercia asked Tamily to care for it, just before she died.'

Anthea looked down at him, a slight frown creasing her forehead.

'Of course I want to do what's right, Dick. But if Tamily is prepared to look after the child, surely that is the obvious solution. We can't very well take a new-born baby to Libya, can we? Or to New Guinea, come to that.'

Dick looked at her anxiously.

'Of course, I realize that, Anthea. We could leave the baby at Allerton while we go to Libya, but we don't have to go to New Guinea. We can alter our plans—take a small house in the country somewhere and give it a proper home.'

She picked up the carved ivory cigarette box and slowly placed a cigarette in the long jade holder. Her movements, as always, were slow and graceful and strangely decisive. Watching her, his heart sinking as the minutes ticked by, Dick knew that she was trying to find a way to let him down kindly. He ought to have known! Deep down inside, he'd known all along that Tammy was right. Anthea wasn't a maternal kind of woman. They'd never discussed the possibility of having a family, but somewhere in the back of Dick's mind he'd supposed that when they were both older they would raise children together in the same happy home atmosphere as that in which he and Mercia and Tamily had grown up. Now the idea seemed ridiculous.

Into his mind came the perfectly clear picture of Tamily in the nursery armchair, in front of a fender obscured by nappies. Try as he might, he could not fill that same chair with a picture of Anthea. He could not even imagine her holding a baby. Those long, pale hands that he had admired could handle a priceless relic with respect and care, but there was no tenderness in her, no warmth. Even those long, strange embraces had been detached and cool. They had aroused in him an urge to conquer that imperturbability; to warm the beautiful cold statue into life. Innocently he had supposed that with marriage, she would change. Now he was suddenly sure that there was no spark to kindle. She was a woman with strong, determined ideas; with a cool, calculating mind, and a passion that encompassed only inanimate objects. There was no joy in nature itself. She would not care that the trees had burst into their spring glory, nor that the sunset was turning the sky to gold. She would not see beauty in the birth of a lamb, nor know the delight in a new-born foal's first stumbling steps. He had been as wrong about her as he had been about Sylvie and Dorice.

Quite suddenly, he knew why he'd made these terrible mistakes.

He had supposed that all women were like the two he knew best in the world, Mercia and Tammy. Stupidly, he had believed that their gentle, loving, generous natures were common to all women; that only the exteriors were different.

He felt a desperate longing to be able to go back to his childhood. He would have liked to find himself suddenly back in the schoolroom, sharing nursery tea with the girls, the upturned 'ludo' board scattered on the carpet, Jess coming in with nursery tea, hot buttered crumpets, doughnuts, and himself carefully cutting the extra slice of cake into three equal portions so that no one should go without.

How simple and uncomplicated life had been! He felt now as he had felt the day he had managed to get lost somewhere in Ten-acre Wood. He'd been seven, or was it eight? Eight surely, for Tamily had been there. Not with him, as she might have been in later years. She was still a shy, quiet, little thing, staying close beside Mercia's chair and blushing every time he spoke to her.

He'd been quite alone in the wood and he'd wandered round in circles until darkness began to fall. He remembered that terrible fear that he might never find his way back, that he would die here, alone in the night, and although he knew his father would send out a search party, he was afraid they wouldn't find him until it was too late.

He'd run blindly down yet another path and then, to his own incredible relief, had found himself in the field. He hadn't stopped running until he reached the

Manor. He'd charged up the stairs, three at a time, flinging open the nursery door and knocking a cup of cocoa out of Jess's hand. She'd scolded him dreadfully, and the girls had giggled. And he'd never been more happy in his whole life.

He stood up abruptly, not realizing that Anthea had still not given him her reply.

'Where are you going, Dick?' she asked in sudden alarm.

He looked so strange. Surely he wasn't going to make an issue of this baby. It would be infuriating if he was going to back out of the expedition at the last minute.

Dick seemed not to see her. He said, tiredly: 'I'm sorry, Anthea. I'm sorry if this upsets you but I can't go through with it. I've made a dreadful mistake. I thought I was in love with you, but I'm not. Please don't be hurt. It's not your fault and it isn't anything to do with the baby, really. Perhaps you could use my sister's unexpected death as a reason to give people for breaking our engagement. I'll go along with any excuse you like to make.'

She was surprised, shocked, and then

angry. She looked at him with cold dislike.

'Get out!' she flung at him, in cool, level tones. 'And don't ever come near my house again...'

TWENTY

Dick burst into the drawing-room regardless of his muddy shoes and the rain dripping off his tweed jacket. Lady Allerton looked up in surprise.

'Where's Tammy?' he asked abruptly.

'I don't know, darling. I haven't seen her all morning. You know, Dick, I'm worried about her. I think this tragedy has affected her much more deeply than we supposed at first. After all that fuss about looking after the baby, she now won't go near it. I think if we're not careful she'll have a nervous breakdown. At breakfast this morning she was as white as a ghost.'

Dick did not stay to hear the rest of his mother's comments. He flung out of the room, across the hall, into the kitchen.

'Cook, where's Miss Tamily?'

'I don't know, Master Dick. Isn't she

upstairs with the bairn?'

Dick turned on his heel and took the stairs three at a time.

He knocked on Tamily's door, but there was no reply. He opened it, glanced round the room once, and closed the door again. On the landing above, Jess was coming out of the nursery suite, the baby wrapped in a white shawl in her arms. With no more than a glance at the child, Dick said:

'Jess, where's Tammy?'

'I don't know, Dick!' she looked at him anxiously. There was a note of urgency in his voice and it worried her. 'Is something wrong?'

'I've got to find her. Haven't you any idea where she could be?'

'I think she said something about taking Cindy for a walk.'

'But it's pouring with rain.'

'Yes, I told her, but I think she went all the same.'

He turned on his heel and swung back down the stairs in the same dangerous way that had brought her heart into her mouth when he was a boy. She heard the garden door slam outside.

What had happened to everyone? It seemed such a short while ago since they were all living here in this beautiful old house, happy and content. Now everywhere she turned there were sorrowful faces and in the night, tears. Even Dick, who should at least have been happy at the prospect of his coming wedding, had looked wild-eyed and distraught. Was this more tragedy coming upon them?

Jess took the baby back into the warm room and rocked it gently against her shoulder. She did not know why Tamily suddenly refused to have anything to do with the child. She had seemed to love it so much, and now she wouldn't even come into the room to watch Jess feed it. She wished she could understand.

Outside in the December rain, Dick strode along beneath the dripping trees, his eyes searching always for Tammy. Once in a while he would stop and whistle for Cindy, knowing his little spaniel would leave even Tammy at his call.

He wondered if she might be down at the farm, perhaps comforting herself with her face against the warm, velvety muzzle of the foal. Wendy whinnied as he pushed upon the stable door, but apart from the foal there was no one else there, no rustle in the hayloft above, where he and Tammy had played hide-and-seek. He closed the door and turned his steps towards Lower Beeches.

The old farmhouse was empty and it was just possible that she had stopped for a while to shelter there from the rain. He felt the damp seeping through the leather shoulder pads of his jacket and soaking into his brogues. He hoped she'd remembered to put on gum boots and a mac.

But the old farmhouse was deserted. Only a few months ago, he and Tamily had forced their way in through the kitchen window where a pane of glass had broken, and built a fire and roasted chestnuts in front of it. That had been their last jaunt before he'd returned to Oxford for the Michaelmas term. There was still a pile of firewood and paper and matches by the grate. He remembered the cheerfulness of the dusty old kitchen in the firelight, and wondered now at its emptiness and chill.

He called her once, hearing her name echo round the empty upstairs rooms. She wasn't here.

For the first time, he began to feel afraid. Supposing he never found her? Supposing he never had the chance to tell her how sorry he was; how selfish he had been; how much he loved her. Supposing she had reached the end of her tether, and decided to put an end to her life. His mother had suggested a nervous breakdown. He remembered Tamily's own words which he had barely noted at the time: 'Why can't you let me have the baby? I've nothing else, Dick.'

He *must* find her. If she wasn't in the house, she had to be somewhere, unless she had gone down to the church. Feeling better now that he had somewhere else to search, Dick hurried off down the muddy footpath and covered the mile to the village in ten minutes. The heavy, studded church door creaked as it swung upon its hinges. The pews were empty. On the altar and round the stained glass windows, the flowers Tamily had arranged for the funeral service were still fresh. But she wasn't here. He went out quickly, forcing himself to walk past the gravestones to find the family vault. The wreaths were the only colour in the whole grey, drear, wet day.

Beneath his feet, a stream of water ran steadily down the path. It gave him one last idea. She might be there. It was the one place he hadn't looked.

Ten-acre paddock was water-logged and the mud squelched beneath his feet as he ran. The rain was driving down so hard now that he could barely see more than a few yards ahead. It was Cindy's excited bark and small drenched form leaping towards him that told him he had found Tamily at last. He called her twice, and then she materialized, silent, ghost-like, behind the sheet of rain. He saw that her head was bare and the dark curls lying flattened by the rain which poured down her face. He couldn't be sure if there were tears, too.

Relief flooded through him. Fear for her sharpened his voice.

'You little idiot!' he said, grabbing her arm. 'You must be mad, being out in this.'

He had to drag her with him across the field. Twilight was falling and through the leafless trees of the spinney, he could see the lights of the Manor glowing, warm and bright. But he wasn't going to take her there. He hurried on beyond the trees, Cindy barking and yapping at their heels. He heard her breathing deeply from the rushed pace he was enforcing, but he did not slow. Presently, the farmhouse loomed close in front of them.

He half-lifted, half-pushed Tamily through the broken window and jumped in after her, relieved at last to be out of the rain. Then he knelt down and within minutes the dry twigs crackled into a blaze. He took off Tamily's wet jacket and pushed her forward near to the fire. He threw on some logs and gradually the warmth spread towards them. Tamily was shivering and her teeth chattered. He took her hands and rubbed them with his own, and after a moment or two the colour began to come back into her cheeks. But he kept hold of her hands.

'Oh, Tammy,' was all he could say, 'Tammy, Tammy!'

She stared back at him, her large brown eyes never leaving his face. She didn't understand. Nothing made sense any more. It had all been too much for her. She couldn't puzzle it out any longer. She was too tired. When Dick had found her, she had thought she would never be able to raise sufficient energy to get home. And it wasn't home any more, anyway. There was nothing in the big house to draw her back, nothing beyond it to draw her away. Life had ceased to have meaning and she had felt completely detached from it all. The sound of Dick's voice calling her hadn't seemed so strange. The first time, she thought she had imagined it. The second time, she walked towards the sound of his voice because somehow, after all, she had nothing else to do.

She didn't know why he had brought her here. Even that didn't seem to be very important. The fire was nice. It was pleasant to be out of the rain. She wondered why Dick was staring at her with that strange look on his face.

'God, how worried I've been, Tammy!' Dick said roughly. 'You really are a silly little fool.'

His words were strangely comforting. That gulf between them had been swallowed up somewhere in the rain and they were close together once more. For the moment, it was more than enough.

'I want to tell you, Tammy. About the baby. She's yours. You can have her.'

Tamily stared back at him, unbelievingly. 'You mean you and Anthea don't want her?'

'I mean she's yours. Mercia gave her to you and she was right. Mercia had the sense to see that you were the one

308

person to whom she could safely trust her child.'

The brief moment of hope faded visibly from Tamily's eyes.

'It's all right, Dick,' she said in a tired voice. 'It was nice of you to make the sacrifice. But I've got used to the idea now. Don't let's talk about it.'

Dick was nearly shaking her with impatience to make her understand.

'Tammy, I *want* you to have her. I want her, too, I want us both to be able to share her. I shall understand if you don't want to marry me.'

Tamily's eyes widened in disbelief.

'Marry you?' she repeated stupidly. In the next moment an explanation for his words came to her.

'I don't see why it's necessary for us to be married. You're her uncle. You would be her guardian. There's no need for us to be married. We can share her without that.'

He *was* shaking her now.

'Tammy, you don't understand. It isn't the baby I'm fighting for, now. It's *you.* Don't you see I've come to my senses at last. I realized today, there in Anthea's flat, that I've never loved her. I've never loved anyone except you. You were so close to me, that I never saw it before. I've been searching all the time for somebody like you...'

He broke off helplessly. How could he make her understand? It had taken him all this long while to see her, not as a very dear sister, but as a young woman whom he admired and respected—and loved. If someone had tried to make him see Tamily in this new light yesterday, no doubt he would have thought them just as mad as Tamily must be thinking him. To Tamily, he was probably still the tiresome elder brother, who teased her, bossed her about and generally made life thoroughly difficult for her. It was a wonder she had put up with him for so long without complaint. If he could only make her understand how humble he felt! If she would only let him, he would spend the rest of his life cherishing her as he knew now she had always cherished him.

Memories were crowding in on him, so fast that they gave him no time for words...—the times she'd got him out of scrapes, the many occasions when she'd slipped him something to eat when his father had sent him up to his room without supper; the long, childish letters she had written to him on his first term at school as if she'd realized how hard it was for a kid of eight to be parted from home for the first time. He had a swift vision of her trailing behind him on expeditions to the 'North Pole'; shivering in the middle of the lily pond, his faithful Man Friday. Tamily painting herself with red-ink spots so they could all avoid a children's party Dick had not wanted to go to; Tamily frantically cobbling the large rent in his pyjama bottoms from sliding down the banisters just after they'd been forbidden to do it again. Tamily trailing up to Oxford to get him out of that wretched mess with Dorice; lending him the cash to buy Sylvie a present...

Appalled, he knew that all his life he had taken from her and never given. With complete egoism he had accepted everything she offered, and as far as he could recall he hadn't always remembered to thank her.

'You've got to forgive me,' he cried desperately.

Tamily did not trust her ears. Had Dick really meant it? Was she light-headed and imagining that Dick had said he loved her?

She dared not let herself hope until she was sure.

'Please, Dick,' she said in the voice of a small, perplexed child, 'Would you say that all again, slowly.'

He caught hold of her shoulder and forced her to look at him.

'Tammy, I love you. I want to marry you. I know I'm not worth a hair of your head but I can't help it. I love you with my whole heart—I always have done.'

She closed her eyes and then opened them again. He was still there, still staring at her with that new strange look in his face. Dick was in love with her—at last, at last it had really happened. With a little cry she flung her arms round him. There was no pretence, no room for artfulness in her love for him.

'Oh, Dick!' she cried, her heart overflowing with happiness. 'Don't you know that I love you? I've always loved you, all my life.'

He put a hand gently beneath her chin and tilted her face upwards, looking down at her in surprise.

'Then you'll marry me, Tammy?'

'Yes, yes,' she breathed her reply. 'Don't you know, darling, that I'd have married you even if you hadn't loved me?'

He gave her that well-remembered teasing smile.

'You always were such a silly little fool!' he said with the deepest tenderness, and a moment later his mouth came down to hers in a long, exultant kiss.

She wasn't cold any more. Her whole being was alight with passionate happiness. She no longer doubted Dick's love for her. That long embrace was all that any woman could desire from the man she loved. In her solitary, hopeless dreams, she had never imagined that she could feel such a wonderful sense of the rightness of things. This was what had been meant for them. Why God had put them here in the world, side by side. She had always known that she could be happy so long as she could love him, but she had never before realized how that happiness was multiplied a thousand times, knowing her love was returned.

Behind them, a log fell from the fire, causing them to jump apart. Dick stooped to put it back in the grate and then turned to her. She saw his face in the light of the bright sparks that were shooting up the chimney, and it was the same face, yet different with the new added qualities of tenderness, and love.

'I know now why I brought you here, and not to the Manor,' he was saying, softly. 'We're going to live here, Tammy, you and I and Mercia's baby. We'll have our own children, too, won't we? Lots of them. We're going to be so very happy. This is our home. It's what you'd like, isn't it darling?'

She nodded, too full of happiness to speak, and there was no need, for Dick had once more gathered her into his arms.

The publishers hope that this book has
given you enjoyable reading. Large Print
Books are especially designed to be as easy
to see and hold as possible. If you wish
a complete list of our books, please ask
at your local library or write directly to:
Dales Large Print Books, Long Preston,
North Yorkshire, BD23 4ND, England.

This Large Print Book for the Partially sighted, who cannot read normal print, is published under the auspices of

THE ULVERSCROFT FOUNDATION

THE ULVERSCROFT FOUNDATION

. . . we hope that you have enjoyed this Large Print Book. Please think for a moment about those people who have worse eyesight problems than you . . . and are unable to even read or enjoy Large Print, without great difficulty.

You can help them by sending a donation, large or small to:

**The Ulverscroft Foundation,
1, The Green, Bradgate Road,
Anstey, Leicestershire, LE7 7FU,
England.**
or request a copy of our brochure for more details.

The Foundation will use all your help to assist those people who are handicapped by various sight problems and need special attention.

Thank you very much for your help.

Other DALES Romance Titles In Large Print

RUTH ABBEY
House By The Tarn

MARGARET BAUMANN
Firefly

NANCY BUCKINGHAM
Romantic Journey

HILDA PERRY
A Tower Of Strength

IRENE LAWRENCE
Love Rides The Skies

HILDA DURMAN
Under The Apple Blossom

DEE SUTHERLAND
The Snow Maiden